*F*igures in
a landscape

00

Barry England

A PALM BOOK

First published by Jonathan Cape 1968

This edition published by Palm Books 1993

Copyright © 1968 Barry England

Design : Mike Rubens 071- 267 3537

Printed and bound by:

The Guernsey Press Co. Ltd

Guernsey, Channel Islands

ISBN 1 898436 02 9

Palm Books Limited

Copyright © the BOOKER prize collection

14 Woodchurch Road London, NW6 3PN

The BOOKER prize collection is one of a new series from Palm Books. The aim is to bring back into print acclaimed novels that have been shortlisted or were winners of the prestigious Booker Prize for Fiction.

"I BELIEVE THAT THE REAL WINNERS OF THE BOOKER PRIZE ARE THOSE ON THE SHORTLISTS."

Bernice Rubens: Winner - 1970 Booker Prize: Judge - Booker Prize 1986

"THE REISSUE OF THESE IMPORTANT NOVELS IS A PUBLISHING ACHIEVEMENT."

Beryl Bainbridge

Barry England was born in 1934, educated at Downside and served for two years as a subaltern in the Far East. After five years as an actor he began writing for the theatre in 1960. Many of his plays have appeared on television. His plays have included "End of Conflict" and the highly successful "Conduct Unbecoming". During his career in the film industry he has written many screenplays, including "The Hill" and is currently writing another screenplay for Hollywood. "Figures in a landscape" was his first novel which was highly commended in the Booker Prize for Fiction shortlist in 1969 and also published in the USA, with

Barry England

excellent reviews - *"A brilliant and moving novel"* ***James Michener*** *"...a tale that rivets one's attention and holds it to the end'"* ***New York Times*** - it was subsequently made into a film. He lives in Royal Berkshire and is currently working on the final draft of a new book.

*F*igures in
a landscape🍎

With their hands tied as usual behind their backs, they had just been paraded through the streets of a small village for the edification of the local population. While they were being formed up for the march to that night's camp, MacConnachie had come suddenly close and whispered harshly:

'If I go left, will you come?'

Ansell, remembering a hundred humiliations at MacConnachie's hands, had stared at him in astonishment.

'What?'

'*Will you come?*'

'Yes.'

'When I move—follow!'

That was the extent of their planning. They had been beaten for talking.

Stumbling along in the fierce heat, Ansell struggled to make his brain think clearly: what have I committed myself to? what have I *done*? His bound arms ached at his back, his anguish of mind feeding on his torment of body. Through glazed eyes he saw MacConnachie look back towards him, and his stomach contracted with fear at the thought of what lay ahead. Not an hour before he had committed himself to a man he feared because that man despised him.

Now one of the Goons screamed at MacConnachie to face his front and MacConnachie swore back. The other prisoners murmured in anger and fear, terrified that MacConnachie

7

would make trouble. MacConnachie spat on them with contempt.

They hate him, Ansell thought. They've all given up, you can see it in the way they shuffle along, heads bent in submission. MacConnachie alone remains stubborn, and they hate him for it. They'd kill him if they could—anything to be rid of that unbending reminder that they were themselves once men.

He is right. We must get away now or we never shall. But how can we hope to survive? And *why pick me?*

It was late afternoon. The prisoners moved raggedly in column of threes along a narrow mountain track, choking on the thick dust that their feet threw up; the weight of the sun pressed constantly over them. The air was suffocating and still, the Goons no less tired or dirty than the men they guarded.

To their right, the massive shoulder of the mountain soared up to a hidden peak; on their left was a sheer drop. Ansell had no idea how deep it was or what lay at the bottom. MacConnachie, he knew, was no better informed than himself since, from the right-hand column, he would have had even less opportunity than Ansell to peer over the edge, and Ansell had had none. He was racked by a terrible sense of having committed himself beyond his capacity; as though, by surrendering to MacConnachie's will, he had made a promise he would be unable to keep. He felt sick with the fear of letting MacConnachie down. Try as he might, he could not feel that he *yearned* for freedom as MacConnachie did, with his entire body. To him it was an idea, however desirable; to MacConnachie, a palpable animal need.

The Goons were all around them, a small group to front and rear, and down each flank a single file of guards keeping pace. All were armed with burp guns. Why in the name of God doesn't he *do* something? Ansell thought. His stomach fluttered in anticipation. He kept remembering the violence in MacConnachie, the crudeness and force, the unpredictability of a man too dangerous to be liked, and his legs trembled at the recurring realization that MacConnachie had chosen him. He is so much the stronger, Ansell thought; he knows the country and he speaks the language. He had that—thing about physical phenomena; that instinct.

What does he need with me?

MacConnachie put his head down, swung left and charged through the ranks of stumbling men, scattering his former comrades in every direction. One of the Goons at the edge of the precipice saw him coming and, alight with fear, struggled frantically to unsling his weapon. MacConnachie dived full length and, catching him in the face with the crown of his head, carried him over, both of them falling from view. Ansell ran forward, shut his eyes, and jumped after them.

For a moment all orientation was lost to him. He tumbled and spun dizzily, completely unaware of what was happening to his body, of whether he fell by the feet or the head. The wind tore at his face, forcing his eyelids apart and his mouth open. He tried to cry out but the echoing din deafened him. He was on the point of vomiting. The next moment he was twisting and turning his trunk in a ludicrous attempt to pull his bottom out through his bound arms. He couldn't breathe. He screamed with terror. Then he hit the water with a stunning crash.

He came to the surface at once, unsure he had ever been under it, and began to pump his back legs with the frantic disorder of a mutilated insect. He had no idea in which direction he was swimming.

'Ansell! Ansell!'

He came suddenly upright and found that he could stand. He started to cough.

'Here!'

MacConnachie was fifteen feet away. He had the Goon's head

trapped between his knees, and was drowning him. The man thrashed about, swimming downwards.

'Find the gun!'

Ansell floundered towards him through the warm, brown water.

'Where is it?'

'I don't know—look for the bastard!'

In a curious, enforced slow motion Ansell danced about, feeling the tacky sludge with his feet, trying to find something hard in all that ooze. MacConnachie rode out a last contortion from the Goon and then released the body, which bobbed a moment and slid from view. Ansell said,

'They're shooting at us.'

'I'm not blind!'

The bullets fell about them with the dead violence of dropped stones, barely breaking the surface of the water as they passed through it. From far above, faint popping noises sounded.

'Here! Over here!'

MacConnachie appeared to have found the gun for, although the churned-up water was impenetrable, he was scowling down at it with fierce attention, slight movements of his head and shoulders indicating that below the surface he was performing some sort of cautious jig. Ansell wallowed over to where he stood.

'Got my right foot under it. See if you can lever it up.'

They faced one another, two men at the centre of a river, with their arms bound tightly behind their backs and bullets all around.

'I can't find it.'

'Put your foot on my leg and follow it down.'

As the toe of Ansell's boot came down MacConnachie's shinbone, he felt the heel knock the gun from the top of MacConnachie's foot.

'You stupid . . .!'

'I've still got my foot on it.'

'Get it underneath—lever it up.'

As he said this, MacConnachie turned his back to Ansell and lowered himself into the water, reaching behind him with groping fingers into the slime. Ansell could feel the metal slithering about on the toe of his boot. Don't let it slip, he prayed, don't let it fall. He eased it up with infinite caution.

'I've got it!'

'Easy, easy ... '

MacConnachie was leaning right back now, only his face above the surface, his hair trailing like weed in the water. This time, it was his water-clumsy fingers that knocked the gun to the bottom again.

'Oh sweet God Almighty!'

In a rage of frustration he turned about, plunged his head down into the filth and reappeared a moment later, the gun clamped between his teeth, his face plastered with muck and slime. This action released a vile stench which rose in bubbles to break on the air.

He grunted frantically until Ansell, interpreting him, turned his back and reached behind him for the gun. The next moment it was in his hands and they were floundering towards the bank, bullets slapping the water all about them.

Then Ansell fell. So great was his anxiety not to let MacConnachie down that he clutched the gun as though it could save him, forgetting to compose his features. Mouth open, breathing in, he swallowed.

His next clear apprehension, moments later, was of being seized by the scruff of the neck and dragged through the shallows, vomiting and retching. Then, at the touch of solid ground, his legs started to function again and MacConnachie, able to open his jaw to release him, shouted,

'Give me the gun!'

'I'm all right!'

But MacConnachie took it and ran for the nearest cover, crouching low. Ansell followed. They fell against the earth and lay there, gasping.

Hunched awkwardly on to his left side, MacConnachie peered up at the mountain. No scent of danger came to him from that direction. In any case, common sense told him that eight hours of heavy downhill labour lay between their late captors and themselves. But on this side of the river he could feel the faint, persistent tug of distant alarm, and he turned his attention to their new territory.

Immediately ahead lay a small area of pimple and scrub. This gave way almost at once to the first slopes of a range of hills that stretched from left to right to fill their entire field of vision with solid undulation. Somewhere beyond these hills, though hidden now by the nearer crests, stood the peaks of a vast mountain range that had become his objective the moment he had sighted them two days before. Once in those mountains, they would have a chance; the initiative would pass from the Goons to them. But first they had to establish their break. Then they had to get there. He rose and said,

'Come on. We must move.'

'Which way?'

'Into the hills. We must be in high ground by nightfall.'

Now that he had recovered, Ansell felt ashamed and frighteningly exposed. He rose and followed MacConnachie with relief.

'Sorry about being sick.'

MacConnachie grunted without interest. He had assumed the poised, characteristic posture that Ansell had seen so often before: the curious animal lope of a man sensing the ground ahead, probing it not only with eyes and ears, but with that strange inner device which Ansell neither possessed nor understood, but which he had learned to envy and trust. Feeling, as he always did, released by this, he began to think ahead, saying,

'What about water?'

'What about it?'

MacConnachie didn't turn but continued to scent the ground ahead, as Ansell himself sought constantly for danger to the flanks and rear.

'We must have some.'

'So?'

'We can't go too far from the river.'

'We've got to get out of the first box of search.'

'There may not be a village up there for miles.'

'There isn't.'

Ansell accepted this without question: if MacConnachie said there was no village, there was none. The fact that MacConnachie had never walked this ground before was immaterial to his particular abilities. Ansell said,

'Then we've got to stay close enough to raid a village down here. There'll be plenty of them on the river.'

For some moments MacConnachie walked on in silence; then he said,

'Damn, you're right.'

Silence fell again. Ansell was unable to discern movement of any kind on any quarter. He found it curious and disconcerting that they should appear, in the circumstances, so utterly alone. He felt threatened. Suddenly MacConnachie pulled violently against his bonds.

'We've got to get our hands free! We've got to!'

'I know.'

They had reached the beginnings of the foot-hills now, and their movements took on a new rhythm as they started to climb.

To the front their field of view was dangerously limited: they could see to a false crest at the top of the slope but, apart from the tips of the hills beyond, nothing more. They walked in the soldier's most ill-starred territory, the low ground, and it made them uneasy. MacConnachie said,

'We'll get to the top. If it isn't crawling with Goons, we'll lie up and come down tonight.'

'Right.'

'We can go without food, but we can't without water.'

The terrain grew steeper until, fifty feet below the crest, they were forced to crawl without the aid of their arms. It was the progress of the snake, and by the time they reached the jutting edge above, their cheeks and knees were raw and bleeding, and what had remained of the arms of their uniform jackets had been torn away. Each man had fragments of crust adhering to the corners of his eyes and mouth, and the foul vapour that rose from their clothes under the late sun choked them.

As they wriggled over the lip of the promontory they found that it was only a small, tufted shelf from which, not ten feet ahead, the slope rose smoothly again to another false crest.

'Oh Christ,' said MacConnachie.

'Quite,' said Ansell, and lay his face in the dirt to rest.

Something had been achieved: looking back, MacConnachie saw that although they had travelled only two hundred yards from the river, their increased elevation had revealed the outskirts of a small fishing village to their left. There was a wooden jetty with one or two native craft lying against it, a handful of villagers in attendance, but, so far as he could see, no sign of danger. He told Ansell to keep watch. Then he settled to examine the cluster of huts. Within moments he had located the village square and, most important, the well. The kid was right. They had to have water. He set his eyes to absorb and fix a plan of the village in his mind. He trusted his eyes, as he trusted every part of his physical mechanism, not to let him down. They were the adjuncts of his instinct; he had no need to think.

After minutes of complete stillness MacConnachie looked at the sky.

'One hour to sunset. Kid, where's that camp?'

'Which one?'

'The one they were marching us to.'

'How would I know?'

MacConnachie looked at him sharply.

'Use your bloody brains! Think!'

'One hour to sunset? We usually get in about eight or nine. That's three hours from the top. Not far, the condition they're in.'

'They'll look for us tonight, then.'

'They might. But with trucks and helicopters, why should they hurry?'

'Um ... look.'

MacConnachie nodded towards the village, indicating it to Ansell for the first time.

'That's handy.'

'We've got to get higher up. We must see forward before we turn back.'

As MacConnachie levered himself upright, the gun clutched awkwardly behind him, Ansell suddenly hissed,

'*Get down!*'

MacConnachie dropped at once.

'What?'

'There's someone coming!'

'Where?'

'Up there!'

MacConnachie wriggled quickly along to the end of the shelf, where he could lay his face against the rising ground and look up the hillside. A civilian Goon was hopping sure-footedly down towards them, turned a little sideways to his own line of march and travelling the steep slope on confident, muscular legs: a fisherman, perhaps, from the near-by village. If he kept to his present course he would land beside them. Keep coming, Mac-Connachie thought; just keep coming.

Ansell came up beside MacConnachie and laid his face close to the big man's. MacConnachie muttered,

'If he'll stop, just long enough, he's a dead man.'

Ansell looked at the Goon, then back to MacConnachie.

'Why?'

The man was closing rapidly.

'Get to the other end of the ledge! Keep hidden!'

There was no time to argue. Stiff with tension, Ansell backed as quickly as he could, never taking his eyes from MacConnachie, one foot against the bottom of the cut to guide him. He saw MacConnachie arch back, drop the gun, and push it out with his foot into the open area of the shelf. MacConnachie then flattened himself into the ground until even Ansell had difficulty in locating his exact position. Ansell did his best to emulate him.

Time passed. They waited. Then they heard the swish of the man's feet through the low scrub. Closer and closer he came until suddenly the feet fell silent. There was a low mutter of surprise and puzzlement. Silence. And then the man jumped down on to the shelf and stood looking at the gun. Clearly he didn't know what to make of it. He looked to left and right and back up the hill. Finally, he crouched to touch it.

MacConnachie rose and kicked him in the side of the head. Perhaps the man felt the blow coming for he half turned and, instead of being stunned, had one eyebrow split open. He screamed as the blood spurted from his forehead. MacConnachie kicked again but the man was falling backwards and the blow caught him in the kidney. The third time MacConnachie kicked him in the groin.

'Come on—finish him!' MacConnachie shouted.

Ansell blundered out at last to join the fight. The man was

screaming repeatedly and now he tried to wriggle forward off the ledge, begging perhaps for mercy. Arms bound tightly behind him, MacConnachie fell awkwardly on top of him, trying to pin the man down by weight alone.

'For Christ's sake, kick him!'

Ansell kicked out at the weaving head. It was a poor shot, catching the man low on the cheek, sending his chin awry but otherwise achieving nothing beyond renewed screaming. He tried again. This time he broke the man's nose and a wild drowning quality was added to the already riveting sounds of his terror. Once more, in sick desperation, Ansell lashed out and caught MacConnachie in the forehead.

'In Christ's name, finish him!' MacConnachie screamed.

Ansell could see that he was barely able to hold the man now, so greatly had pain and the fear of death increased his strength. They were being carried together, in their locked struggle, towards the lip of the shelf. Ansell took careful aim and drove his foot at the head once more; the teeth crumbled inwards under his toe. The man screamed and screamed and would not die. Ansell lost control. He kicked and kicked until, at the third blow, he felt the man's temple give a little under the impact, and at last he fell silent.

'Is he dead?'

'Oh God. Oh sweet Christ in heaven.'

MacConnachie hauled himself upright, calculated the position of the head, and stove in the skull wall with two carefully judged blows from his loaded toe-caps.

'He is now.'

Ansell wandered off a little, turned, and crouched against the cut of the shelf.

'I'm going to be sick.'

MacConnachie rocked his head back and forth in outrage and a sort of grief.

'Messy killing,' he cried. 'God, I hate messy killing!'

Ansell found that he had no urge whatever to vomit; nothing came. Roughly, MacConnachie said, 'Come on.'

Ansell joined him.

Back to back, they dragged the body to the rear of the shelf and stripped it. Under the first layer of clothing they found, tucked into a pouched belt, a fish knife with a thin, sharp, eight-inch blade.

'That's why we killed him,' MacConnachie said. Ansell said nothing. MacConnachie reached behind him, drew out the knife and said, 'Lean towards me.'

The next moment Ansell's hands became separated for the first time in days. He turned at once to release MacConnachie. Then they sat, both of them in silence, glorying in the free movement of their arms, caressing their bruised and rope-burned wrists. MacConnachie had actually to peel one section of rope out of his flesh, where it had eaten its way in and embedded itself. This left a raw, shallow channel in the meat.

MacConnachie said, 'Take the gun. Keep watch.'

As he stood on guard, Ansell glanced every now and then at MacConnachie to see what he was doing. First, he removed the dead man's belt. Then he rolled his clothes into a neat bundle, tying them together with the sleeves of the native coat. Finally, he went through the pouches of the belt. There was a slim bundle of notes in the first. 'About five bobs' worth,' said MacConnachie. And nothing in any of the others until he came to the last. He withdrew a tiny object, and said,

'What the hell's this? Looks like a chicken's beak.'

'Probably a lucky charm.'

'Well, it didn't do him much good,' said MacConnachie, and tossed it aside. Ansell found that he was disturbed by this. He said,

'We could leave it with him.'

'He hasn't got any pockets. What shall I do? Shove it up his jacksi?'

Ansell said nothing. MacConnachie said,

'He's coming with us, anyway.'

'*Coming with us?*'

'Watch your front!'

MacConnachie rose, strapped the belt round his own waist, tied the bundle of clothes to it, slipped the knife under it, and said,

'I don't want him found before nightfall. After that, we'll dump him. Till then, he comes too.'

He bent and raised the body with one hand under each armpit until it stood upright. He looked to Ansell and said, 'Come on. Fireman's carry.'

Obediently, Ansell crossed, stooped, thrust one arm between the dead legs and, as MacConnachie lowered the weight of the corpse across his shoulders, took hold of a dead wrist with the same hand. MacConnachie then took the gun, leaving Ansell's other hand free for balance and support. Ansell said,

'He's still warm.'

'He'll stay that way a long time in this heat. Let's move.'

They set off up the hill, two men, three bodies.

Just before they left, when Ansell's back was turned, Mac-Connachie had crouched, retrieved the chicken's beak, and returned it surreptitiously to the pouch. Now he led the way forward.

With their arms free, the going was much easier. Although the slope was no less steep, there were occasional bushes to pull upon, and a well-worn path to follow. MacConnachie saw no point in avoiding it. The lie of the land was such that, should anyone appear over the horizon, the encounter would turn on which of them moved first; and MacConnachie was confident that he would. He was quicker to react than anyone he had come against.

Twice he fell back to relieve Ansell, the second time keeping the body, for Ansell had begun to labour badly. He retained the gun also, seeing that Ansell was in no condition to use it. He settled for the watch on their rear that Ansell could still provide.

Three times they struggled up the last slopes of a crest, only to find that the land had deceived them, and they were forced to move on again. MacConnachie said,

'It'll be like this. We might as well get used to it.'

On the last occasion Ansell nodded, hunched his shoulders and, with drooping head, trudged across to take up the corpse once more. MacConnachie remained silent; he was himself weary, and to express surprise or admiration was alien to him. They moved on. The sun was low in the sky now and every feature cast a long shadow. The tension of their escape had left them. Whatever they did hurt.

At the next crest they were lucky. They looked down into a gully broad enough to constitute a defensible position. While Ansell sank to his knees, letting the corpse roll off his back, Mac-Connachie went forward to examine the terrain.

The gully was sixty feet across, its floor split by fissures seven or eight feet deep. Beyond its farther side the hill rose up sharply to a feature so high it could only be the first crest of the range proper. From MacConnachie's left, a single spar of sunlight pierced a saddle to paint its upper edges in gold. While daylight lingered in the high country it was night already in the valleys, and where he stood the heavy shadows gathered fast. He crossed to one of the fissures and peered down into it.

'All right, we can chuck him in this one.'

Ansell, who had been staring at the dead face as though to reanimate it, rose, seized the corpse by the heels, and dragged it down to where MacConnachie stood. He was about to topple it over when MacConnachie said, 'Wait a minute.'

With every appearance of embarrassment MacConnachie

fumbled the beak out of the pouch, stooped, and wrapped the lifeless fingers round it.

'That's our luck,' he growled. 'Not his. *Ours!*'

And he sent the body over with a short heave. Ansell said,

'You're whistling in the dark.'

MacConnachie said,

'Get stuffed.'

Ansell wandered over to the next crack, and relieved himself. MacConnachie, apparently satisfied that the corpse was sufficiently hidden, did the same.

They settled into a small depression just below the skyline. MacConnachie stripped the gun down and did his best to clean it. After a moment, he said,

'We must find something to oil this damned thing with, or it'll rust to hell.'

But Ansell was preoccupied and failed to reply. The night closed slowly about them. Later, Ansell said,

'It was incredible how long he took to die.'

MacConnachie grunted, his attention fixed on the breech-block. Ansell continued,

'You get used to killing from farther away. You forget.'

'It's not easy to kill a man without a weapon.'

'No.'

MacConnachie looked at him.

'If we hadn't killed him, we'd still have our hands tied behind our backs.'

'He might not have been carrying a knife.'

'You pays your money, and you takes your choice. You can't raid a village with your hands tied up. You can't rob a man either. You kill him, or you leave him alone. We killed him, and we're free.'

'In a manner of speaking.'

'That's right.'

MacConnachie began to reassemble the weapon. Ansell said, 'What happens now?'

'We move to a position from which we can see the village. When we're ready, we go in.'

'How soon?'

'Not later than midnight.'

'That's too early.'

'We can't wait. We've got to be in, out, and as far as we can by dawn.'

'Will we be out of the first box of search by then?'

'No.'

Ansell took a breath, and asked the question he had hesitated to ask until this moment.

'How far have we got to go?'

MacConnachie operated the working parts of the gun, clipped on the magazine and rose before he replied.

'About four hundred miles.'

'That far?'

'That far.'

From their new position they could see what few lights still burned in the village. A café of some sort remained open, a fierce glare escaping from its farther side, where a lamp would be hanging at the door. Every now and then a figure emerged to cast an elongated shadow down the street. But apart from this, and perhaps a dozen other isolated glimmers at slatted windows, the village lay dark.

The well was situated in a square that opened out from the main street. The surrounding buildings were all of wood—low, rickety-looking huts. The place had a temporary, tacked-together look, as though it might be abandoned tomorrow to leave a dark, rotting stain on the neat fields that hedged it about, palely glowing in the soft light which transfused the entire area.

MacConnachie said,

'We'll go in, one up, one down, along the main track. Any-where near those fields we'll show like a shilling on a sweep's arse.'

'I agree.'

'First we want water—and something to carry it in. Then food. Anything small that'll last. Chocolate, sugar, tinned stuff. Finally whatever we can use. Tools, waterproofs, money—and some-thing to carry that in, too. A haversack, if possible. That's very important.'

'Right.'

'I'll wear the Goon clothes and carry the knife; you take the gun. Cover me as deep as you can. If anything comes up, I'll deal with it. Don't interfere unless you have to. And don't use the gun unless we start a war.'

'Right.'

'Blacken up now, and tear off any hanging bits of cloth.'

While MacConnachie stripped off his trousers and added them to the bundle at his waist, Ansell scraped up a handful of dirt, mixed it into a paste with spittle, and smeared it over his fore-head and cheeks. But when, having torn off two or three strips of dangling sleeve, he made to throw them aside, MacConnachie said, 'No, put them in your pocket. They may come in useful and I don't want to leave a trail.' Finally, MacConnachie pulled the full-length native coat over his jacket and blackened his own face. He still had his boots on and Ansell laughed.

'You look like a navvy dressed up as a nun.'

MacConnachie's teeth gleamed for a moment. He said,

'If you want to pee, now's the moment.'

Then he handed the gun to Ansell and drew the knife, saying,

'We'll r/v at the tree, right-hand bottom corner of the square. You see it?'

'Yes.'

'Let's go.'

'Good luck.'

In twenty minutes they reached the edge of the fields, Mac-Connachie walking upright, Ansell tracking him at fifty feet distance. A cool breeze had sprung up. MacConnachie looked back a moment, and smiled. In all this time he had caught no single glimpse of Ansell. The boy didn't know it, but he had a gift for assimilating natural cover as remarkable as any Mac-Connachie had seen; he was a born stalker. Of course it was MacConnachie who was the born killer so that, for the moment, Ansell's gift was supportive rather than assertive. But since Mac-Connachie appreciated it, and knew how to make use of it, its value was assured.

He turned and walked up the track towards the village.

Ansell followed, somehow remaining, despite the relative brightness of the fields, invisible against their separating banks.

Ten minutes more, and MacConnachie had reached the scrub that bordered the village. He dropped from view. Ansell closed the gap to five yards. He could just make out the figure of Mac-Connachie ahead of him, lying full length and peering between the huts. He checked once more to their flanks and rear and adopted the same position.

They lay at the point where the track entered the village to become its main street. A hundred yards along this street, the square opened out to the left. The café was on the right, another thirty yards farther up, the glare from its pressure lamp still flaring harshly back against the buildings to the edge of the square. This was a danger they could do nothing about, since to attempt to put it out would create a greater hazard than leaving it alight.

Among the huts a dog whined.

MacConnachie rose and signalled that he was going up the right-hand side of the street. Ansell acknowledged; then held himself tightly against the moment that always occurs at the outset of such an operation when the striker, on first emerging from his hide, seems to scream for attention as though floodlit, and his cover man has to choke back a cry of warning. The moment passed, and Ansell ran quickly and lightly to the corner round which MacConnachie had disappeared.

The street was deserted. MacConnachie was working his way up to the right in well-judged breaks from cover to cover. He looked purposeful and calm. Ansell waited until a gap of twenty feet had opened up and then he too moved out into the street, slipping from shadow to shadow in MacConnachie's wake, maintaining distance and stalking him. Thus for fifty yards they progressed undisturbed. Then a man came out of the café and weaved his way towards them. He didn't appear too badly drunk since, apart from the occasional explosive belch, he remained blessedly silent, bent, it seemed, solely on getting his legs to bed. Ansell reversed the gun to use as a club; MacConnachie he knew would be holding the knife low and close, the blade ready. But the man, utterly oblivious of their presence, passed stiffly within a few feet of them, entered one of the huts, exchanged curses with the voice of a woman and fell silent. MacConnachie looked back and shrugged cheerfully. Then, for fifteen minutes, they stood without moving until the sense of stillness came over them again.

Once more, MacConnachie led the way forward. They had just reached a point from which both could look out across the square, MacConnachie now no more than a yard from the tree, when the second man came out of the café.

This one was falling-down drunk. He lurched and plunged about the garishly lit street as though in pursuit of his own monstrous shadow. Yet he too remained silent, mainly, Ansell suspected, because to open his mouth would be to invite disaster; he carried himself with the air of a man constantly on the point of vomiting. An amused shout came after him and then the light diminished. Clearly the proprietor, having rid himself of his last customer, had taken the lamp inside.

Baffled by this sudden dimness the man reached out for support, fell sideways, and clung to the tree not two feet from where MacConnachie stood. It seemed impossible to Ansell that he should fail to see the other figure. Nor did he, for, with a little cry of pleasure, the man released the tree and staggered forward to embrace MacConnachie. Ansell waited for him to stiffen in surprise as the knife went in. Instead, arms about one another, they muttered for some moments and then, throwing back their heads, roared with laughter. Ansell was electrified with astonishment and fright; but MacConnachie, apparently unaware of any danger, continued the conversation at the top of his voice until, with a vigorous display of back-slapping, he sent the man on his way across the square.

This unlooked-for friendliness in the night appeared to have restored the man's confidence, for he progressed now with unwarranted bravado, turning every few yards to wave back and shout at MacConnachie, who returned the salutation. At length, two thirds of the way across the square, he turned for one last exchange of good wishes and fell down the well.

This was no more than a sunken bath four feet square, its water level only inches below that of the street. But it became rapidly apparent that the drunk was unable to extricate himself and would surely drown. Between gaspings and thrashings about he was making a great deal of noise. MacConnachie swore. 'Wait here!'

Hardly believing his eyes, Ansell watched as MacConnachie fled across the square, dragged the man out, thumped him and carried him quickly from view behind the corner of a hut. The next moment MacConnachie was running back alone, signalling to Ansell to join him at the tree.

'I don't want to waste any more time. He's out for the night. See if we can find something to carry water in.'

They turned to the nearest huts and were lucky at once. From a nail in one of the wooden uprights hung a large, flat, circular canteen on a canvas strap. It was eighteen inches across, nearly as tall, and four inches deep. It seemed inconceivable that anyone should leave so valuable a possession unguarded, for it must hold close to twenty pints of water. When Ansell pointed it out to him, MacConnachie muttered, 'I don't believe it.'

But it was there all right; and so, close at hand, was an old woman sitting on a stoop, who must have watched everything that had so far transpired without uttering a sound. At her feet lay the body of a dead man, a son perhaps, or a grandson. She seemed to be aware of them and yet divorced from their actions, as though she looked both at and through them. For some moments they returned her gaze in a state of shocked suspension. Ansell felt a prickle of weird unreality. Then MacConnachie walked across, took down the canteen and shook it; Ansell could tell that it contained water and was sound. MacConnachie came back and stared down at the old lady. Apparently satisfied that whatever ritual of mourning she was performing she constituted no danger to them, he handed the canteen to Ansell and said,

'Refill it, fresh water entirely. Then drink what you want, quickly!'

'Right.'

'Leave the gun, here's the knife.'

Ansell ran quickly to the well, crouched, laid down the knife and, removing the stopper from the canteen, poured its contents into the dust. As soon as it was empty he plunged it below the surface and waited impatiently for it to refill; then he withdrew it, stoppered it tightly, looked about him, and plunged his face into the well to drink his fill. He found to his surprise that he didn't enjoy it. As soon as he started to drink he was attacked by an outbreak of wind; and his thirst, strangely, had left him. But, spacing his gulps, he did his best to replace the liquid lost during the day; then, knife in one hand and canteen, unexpectedly heavy now, in the other, he ran back to MacConnachie.

While MacConnachie drank, Ansell kept watch, the absolute

stillness of the old lady making him, for no reason, acutely uneasy. He had the feeling that they no longer controlled events. MacConnachie returned, took the gun, and said,

'We might as well try this hut first.'

But now the old lady rose in muted protest, barring the way; this, it appeared, she would not allow. MacConnachie murmured, 'Sorry, love,' and struck her down with a short, right-arm chop. Catching at the front of her clothing, he sat her gently against the door jamb and passed inside. Hesitating, Ansell followed.

There was one room with a yard at the back. It may have been that gifts had been brought in recognition of the visitation of death. Whatever the explanation, there were little piles of food neatly laid out all over the table and bed: fish, fruit, vegetables and some flowers. Not much of this was useful to them but, stuffing fruit into their pockets and munching as they worked, they searched the room. In a cupboard Ansell came on an unexpected hoard of tins, four of meat and two of soup. There were also two jars of paste, a small quantity of sugar and a larger amount of salt. Since the sugar tin lacked a lid, MacConnachie told him to add the sugar to the salt, which he did. MacConnachie then displayed his own discovery, laughing.

'Look what I found under the bed.'

It was a small, shabby suitcase tied up with a piece of rope.

'Surely we can do better than that?'

But MacConnachie said, 'It'll do for the time being,' and proceeded to pack their plunder into it, adding a sharp kitchen knife and the rough blanket from the bed which, stuffed in tight, held the rest of it together. Finally he roped up the case, took a native coat from a peg on the wall and tossed it to Ansell, saying,

'Put it on. He won't need it where he's gone.'

When he was ready, Ansell said,

'Where now? The café?'

'I reckon.'

They had intended to approach the café with stealth, do a recce, leave the suitcase and canteen and go in with knife and gun. But whatever good fortune had guided them to the canteen now deserted them. For they were still twenty feet from the back entrance when a dog started to bark with a loud, vicious and dangerous persistence. At once the lamp, which had previously glowed in the front of the building, moved hurriedly through to the rear. MacConnachie swore, and whispered urgently,

'We'll have to back off!'

'But we need the stuff in there.'

'We can't fight the dog!'

'We can kill it!'

'Not with the gun, and any other way we might get bitten!'

'Well, for Christ's ... '

'Shut up!'

The proprietor had appeared on the back porch, holding out the lamp from side to side and shouting at the dog to be quiet. Eventually he subdued it with a sharp kick on the muzzle, and then called out into the darkness while the dog whined and growled and pulled at its chain. After a moment or two, he grunted with annoyance, swore at the dog, slammed back into the café and bolted the door. The dog continued to snarl, its hair standing up as it glared in their direction. Ansell whispered crossly,

'What does it matter if we get a bit of a bite?'

'You can never trust an animal to be clean. We go back.'

Bad-temperedly, Ansell followed MacConnachie. Once they were in the room again he burst out furiously,

'So what the hell do we do now?'

MacConnachie was just as angry.

'Haven't you ever heard of rabies?'

'He wouldn't keep a rabid dog.'

'How the hell would you know?'

'For God's sake!'

'Look—we take no unnecessary chances. Not as long as we're in this place and we've still got a chance to get something out of it. We've a long way to go! Right?'

Sulkily, Ansell said,

'All right.'

'So trust me.'

'So what do we do?'

MacConnachie looked at him. After a moment, he said,

'I don't know. You tell me.'

But Ansell was calmer now and his brain had started to function. He said,

'The first drunk ... '

'What about him?'

'He'll take a bit of waking.'

'Can you remember which house?'

'Yes.'

'Let's go.'

No word of thanks; no acknowledgement. Ansell said,

'Shall I bring the suitcase?'

'Of course.'

Outside, Ansell stooped to check on the old lady, who was deeply unconscious. MacConnachie hissed at him,

'I don't make mistakes. Come on!'

At the edge of the square they checked all round their field of view: silence, stillness. MacConnachie said,

'Which one?'

Ansell counted down the houses on the other side of the street.

'The seventh.'

'Right. I'll go in with the knife. You take everything else, cover me from across the street. When I signal, join me.'

Ansell waited until a gap of fifteen feet had opened up and then he followed MacConnachie down what was, to them, now the left-hand side of the street. With the canteen round his neck, the gun in one hand and the suitcase in the other, and with the skirts of his long coat brushing about his ankles, he felt ridiculous trying to be stealthy. All was quiet.

Opposite the house, MacConnachie paused. Ansell unslung the canteen, put down the suitcase and crouched in a firing position. He watched as MacConnachie flitted across the street in the pale light, but then lost him in the shadows at the side of the hut. For ten minutes nothing happened and the village was absolutely still.

Then a darker shadow appeared in the front of the building as the door opened. Ansell gathered up their possessions and ran to join MacConnachie. As soon as he was inside, MacConnachie shut the door and whispered, 'Quiet!'

In the first hut there had been some light reflected from the café. Here it was pitch dark. Ansell waited for night vision to come. Suddenly he screwed up his eyes as light flared directly beneath them: MacConnachie had struck a match and was lighting a candle-end at a table. Ansell went forward to remonstrate, but MacConnachie gestured him to silence. When he had screened the candle with a vase from the far end of the room, MacConnachie came close and put his lips to Ansell's ear.

'We've got to take a chance. It's after one. Search as quick and quiet as you can. They're asleep at the other end.'

Ansell's eyes were growing accustomed to the flickering light and he saw now that, in one case at least, 'asleep' was something of a euphemism. The woman lay sprawled half out of bed, a patch of blood showing at her left ear. She breathed heavily. Her husband, for different reasons, was equally stertorous beside her. MacConnachie said,

'See if you can find more matches, and some oil for the gun.'

They set to work. Their swift, silent search uncovered one tin of condensed milk; an old safety razor which Ansell would have rejected, but which MacConnachie added firmly to the contents of their case, now open on the table; a tin of some sort of grease which MacConnachie sniffed, tasted, and elected also to keep; a narrow bottle of vegetable oil, almost empty, with a little of which MacConnachie immediately oiled the accessible working parts of the gun; one box of eleven matches, and one of seven; another candle; a little more sugar, which went into their tin; and some money, which MacConnachie added to that already in his belt.

It wasn't good. Most disturbing of all, they still lacked any alternative to the suitcase. MacConnachie was clearly concerned about this. He repacked their belongings, snuffed the candle and put it into his jacket pocket. Then he came to Ansell and said very quietly,

'We'll have to try another hut.'

This, Ansell knew, went against all MacConnachie's instincts, for, to do so, they would have to steal time from the other end of the night, when they would most need it. He waited quietly for MacConnachie to lead the way.

MacConnachie went to the door and opened it. As if on cue, there came a piercing shout from the direction of the square. After a moment of silence it came again, startlingly clamorous, and then once more. Ansell closed up to look over MacConnachie's shoulder. He saw the door of the café open, and then the proprietor come running out, pressure lamp held high. At the edge of the square he encountered the shouting man, who proved to be the second drunk, the one MacConnachie had rescued from the well. Despite MacConnachie's assurance, the man was clearly conscious and vocal.

'Oh Christ, I should have let the little bastard drown.'

'Do we go and sort them out?'

'No, you never know who'll turn out to be a hero.'

By this time the drunk and the proprietor were berating one another at the tops of their voices, and lights had appeared at two other windows. Now the woman in bed behind MacConnachie

and Ansell started to moan at the first return of awareness, and
MacConnachie said,

'We'll have to bug out.'

'I'll cover you.'

'No, together. They're not interested in us.'

It was true; for, as MacConnachie and Ansell fled lightly down
the street, the quarrelling men did not look once in their direction; and they were already beyond the scrub and on to the
track before they heard the woman scream.

It had not been a successful raid. They had saved one life,
bent two heads, and stolen sufficient water. But they lacked
everything else that they needed to survive. No drugs, no soap,
no medicines; too little food and money; no waterproofs, no
tools and no haversack. And they had, if MacConnachie's guess
was correct, four hundred miles to go.

It took an hour to reach the gully again, and here they rested
for five minutes. MacConnachie stripped down the gun and
oiled it properly, while Ansell sat recovering his breath. At length,
Ansell said,

'We didn't do very well.'

'It's a start.'

Ansell kicked the suitcase.

'The trouble is, we'll have to carry this damned thing. We
can't sling it.'

'I know.'

Then Ansell chuckled.

'You realize we haven't got a tin opener.'

'We've got a couple of knives.'

'Not to mention a cut-throat razor.'

'We'll use that tomorrow.'

'We're going to *shave*?'

'Not our faces. Armpits and crutches.'

'You're joking!'

'You won't laugh if you get the rot.'

'I shan't laugh if the razor slips, either.'

'I'll do it for you, if you like.'

'No thanks. You look after your inheritance, I'll look after mine.'

Now MacConnachie laughed. Then he reassembled the gun, tested its action, and stood up.

'I'll take the lead with the suitcase and gun. You bring the canteen.'

'Right.'

'We go as far as we can. An hour before dawn, we rest.'

'Amen.'

'It won't hit us properly till the day after tomorrow.'

'I like to have something to look forward to.'

They marched steadily throughout the remainder of the night, sometimes climbing, sometimes descending, the one by no means easier than the other. From time to time they swopped suitcase for canteen, but these periods grew longer for MacConnachie, mostly in charge of the suitcase, and shorter for Ansell, who seemed most often to carry the canteen. If they had anything in their favour, it lay in the fact that they were still making their initial outlay of strength. From the morning, when they would be forced to make a second start, there would follow a period of adjustment to their new condition which would be physically painful and psychologically difficult. On top of this, they would have to combat the effects of an imprisonment which had involved, besides the customary severe confinement, a deliberate policy of physical debilitation, the aim of which had been to render them, through the deprivation of food, sleep, sanitation and elementary comfort, fit subjects for re-education. MacConnachie had been right to suppose that they must escape quickly, or not at all.

Fortunately, on this first night, the hills proved soft, and they concentrated simply on maintaining a dull, steady rhythm. At length they reached a height from which, in MacConnachie's estimation, they would have a reasonable view to front and flanks, and here they rested. MacConnachie was asleep before Ansell.

MacConnachie came awake quickly as dawn was on the point of breaking, and watched the sun come up. Until the daylight had moved into the low ground, he remained absolutely still, examining every inch of the unfolding landscape. He saw no one, nor did he expect to. Only later would the search begin, and when it did it would be a full-scale operation, involving every device and unit that the Goons could deploy. He and Ansell had killed a guard; they were therefore 'armed and dangerous'. They had an hour's grace and must make full use of it.

Ahead, there was a narrow depression rising to a gentle slope that extended all the way to the crest of the highest feature they had yet faced. To flanks and rear, the foot-hills lay back in mild undulation to the river. Once satisfied that they could not easily be approached from any direction, he woke Ansell.

'We'll just eat fruit this morning; we had a good meal in the hut last night and I want to save the tins.'

'Okay.'

'First we shave, then we check our gear, then we go.'

'Right.'

While Ansell undressed, munching an apple, MacConnachie stropped the razor against his boot. Each in turn then shaved off his own body hair with the dry razor. As they did so, they talked.

'Everything depends on how many units there are this side of the river, between us and the mountains.'

'There'll be dozens, surely?'

MacConnachie frowned.

'There'll be one or two within thirty miles, and a dozen others somewhere in these hills—all within striking distance.'

'You want to use this on your throat?'

But MacConnachie didn't smile.

'The most important thing is not to be seen. The choppers will be up soon. The moment they spot us, they've got a chance to recapture us. *We must keep out of sight.*'

'How do you want to play it?'

'If we get warning, hide. Otherwise, freeze.'

As soon as the shaving was done, MacConnachie set about his inspection in assessment of their readiness to travel. First the canteen. It was of solid construction, decorated with great elegance and in perfect condition.

'It's beautiful,' said Ansell. 'Look at that chasing round the neck.'

'It holds water,' said MacConnachie.

'What is it? Leather-covered brass?'

'Probably. The point is, it won't reflect sunlight.'

Then the suitcase.

'I don't see any way to fix a strap on this. The rope's too short, and the material's too crappy.'

'It's cardboard, I think, with artificial leather on the outside.'

'It'll have to do. Can you repack it in some sort of order?'

Ansell did so. First he emptied it entirely. Then he folded the blanket into one long narrow strip. This he laid across the open case, pressing the centre of the material down until it was flush with the bottom and sides of the interior, the blanket ends still protruding to left and right for about a foot. Into this nest he repacked their possessions. He then turned to MacConnachie.

'What do we wear for travelling?'

'The Goon clobber. Pack the jackets and slacks for night time.'

But the slacks wouldn't go in, the jackets having filled the remaining space.

'Doesn't matter,' said MacConnachie, 'we'll tie 'em round our waists.'

Ansell finished the job by folding the blanket ends over the jackets, shutting the case and tying it tightly with the rope. Now they had only to open the lid and turn back two flaps to get at whatever they wanted.

Finally MacConnachie inspected their boots, their bodies and the gun.

Their boots were in reasonable condition. Most of the studs had gone, but neither pair was perforated at sole or heel, and in each case the uppers were firmly attached all round. They were fortunate in that, so long as the Goons had still to march them, they were forced to leave them shod. Without boots now, they would be finished.

Neither man had been deeply cut during the preceding day's climb. They used a little water to wash their faces and hands, and trusted to luck in the matter of healing. Ansell, however, insisted on binding one of the torn-off sleeves round MacConnachie's damaged left wrist.

'Oh, for God's sake!' said MacConnachie.

'I don't want you losing your left hand,' said Ansell. 'Someone's got to carry the case and I don't fancy it.'

'Get on with it, then, don't yatter!'

For a third time, MacConnachie stripped the gun and satisfied himself that it was thoroughly oiled and fully operative. An unreliable gun was, to MacConnachie, the equivalent of a missing limb. He emptied the magazine and refilled it.

'Twenty-five rounds. I'm setting the gun on single-shot. It's your job to check it night and morning; see it stays that way.'

'Right.'

MacConnachie rose.

'We travel one up, one down, as before. You're in charge of

the canteen and the knife. I carry the gun and the suitcase. We each have one mouthful of water before we start.'

'Okay.'

'We eat tonight, and once each dawn and dusk. Water at midday, if we need it, but we'll try to do without.'

Ansell unscrewed and withdrew the stopper, which was attached to the neck of the canteen by a fine chain. Each man savoured and drank one mouthful of water, then Ansell restoppered the canteen and hung it over his shoulder. They were ready to move. MacConnachie said,

'Watch for planes. I'm relying on you.'

'Right.'

MacConnachie estimated the distance to the mountains at seven days' march. It was here, in the hills, that the greatest danger lay; and here, logically, that the Goons would most like to encounter them.

Coming down from the hills, they should find a valley. Mac-Connachie believed it would be watered, and therefore inhabited, and it was at that point that he planned to replenish their stores before tackling the mountains.

There was one small danger at their backs: the Goons from whom they had escaped would send a force across the river in pursuit, and thus the rear would always be closed to them. But he believed they could remain permanently ahead of this party and, shutting his mind to further thought, he sent his instinctual scouts to probe the territory before him.

The first plane came without warning. They were just short of the initial crest when there was a whoosh, a flash of shadow, and it was gone, scudding away beyond the ridge. They hadn't time even to pause in their stride. MacConnachie said,

'That was chance. They wouldn't send jets after us. Too fast, too little visibility.'

'Ignore it, then?'
'Yes. Keep going.'

Beyond the crest, the ground fell away over half a mile into an area of hillocks, pimples and scrub, rising gradually thereafter for nearly two miles to what appeared to be the main spine of the entire hill range. MacConnachie did not believe it. It simply didn't tie in with his estimated distance to the mountains. He knew at once that there must be two main spines to the range, both running across their front, and roughly parallel to one another. This meant, in effect, that he and Ansell would have to scale the range twice. It didn't double the distance, but it doubled the effort. He glanced back at Ansell, then swore softly to himself.

It was when they were down low, in the worst possible position from the point of view of visibility, still pushing their way through the pimples and scrub, that Ansell thought he heard the second plane. He stopped and called, 'Listen!'

MacConnachie, too, stopped, and both concentrated all of their sensory perception into their ears. After a moment or two, they heard the unmistakable swishing cut of helicopter blades.

'Chopper!'

'Yes. About a mile away.'

'Could be less. Damn.'

'Do we hide, or press on?'

'I don't like being stuck down here.'

They were enclosed on all sides, most severely to the front and left. MacConnachie pointed to a scar that ran up the main feature just right of their line of march.

'We'll go up that,' he said, and set out. Ansell followed. He could see that the scar was well grown with brush, and would provide some cover when the time came. He said,

'The chopper'll be doing a box search, going back almost as far as it comes forward. We should get a fair way up.'

39

'He'll be well ahead of the infantry, too. They'll try to spot us first, then fly the Goons in to catch us.'

The scar proved a much different proposition close to. The scrub was tight-knit, difficult to climb through, and the earth, more powdery than Ansell had suspected, threw up choking billows of dust. With the blazing sun well up in the sky now, and heat coming back at them from the ground, they began to sweat profusely as they scrabbled upwards, bent double, clutching at the rough growth for leverage. Ansell, glimpsing MacConnachie, saw that progress was doubly difficult for him, since he had the case as well as the gun to deal with. The solution he had arrived at was to tuck the case under his gun arm, leaving the other free to claw with; but this sent him constantly floundering to knees or stomach as his boots skidded over the brush and support failed him. Ansell's own discomfort was compounded by the need to look constantly over his shoulder for a sight of the helicopter. After twenty minutes, he saw it.

'*Freeze!*'

He knew from the immediate silence that MacConnachie was holding himself rigidly in whatever position the order had caught him. Ansell himself watched the chopper's manoeuvring, peering through the heat and dust, trying to shield any glare from his face with a hunched shoulder.

The helicopter slid lazily to left and right across their line of march, an insect tasting the air for a scent of its prey. At the moment it was also moving forward but he knew that if he waited it would dance back to complete the box it was engaged on, before advancing again into the next square pattern. He could hear no other rotors, which suggested that the Goons were short of air power and, unable to work overlapping boxes of search, were spreading the net as wide as they could until they unearthed a specific trail. How right MacConnachie had been to say that invisibility was everything.

At length the helicopter fell back below the last crest, and Ansell shouted up to MacConnachie,

'All clear! Let's hide!'

'Left! Go left!' MacConnachie called back, starting to wriggle in that direction. Ansell could see that just above them the scrub grew thicker to that side, and he burrowed after MacConnachie deep into the crackling brush. They settled face down, hidden from one another but only three feet apart, waiting for the chopper to return. With the baked earth so close to his cheeks, and the brush packed tight about him, Ansell began to feel acutely claustrophobic in the heat, tormented by the dust that caught at his throat and prickled in his nostrils. With infinite caution, he readjusted his position so that he would be able to look at the sky. He had discovered months before that, so long as he was able to make tiny movements of this kind, he could hold back the build-up of pressure out of all proportion to the size of the movement itself. Somewhat comforted, he waited.

The helicopter came back, and the swishing sounds cut deep into the shallows around them. For far too long the search went on, the machine floating above them, slipping sideways, floating again, passing over and above and below their position a dozen times, never leaving their field of vision, persistently a danger to them. Ansell could hear MacConnachie cursing and shifting restively. He knew why. So long as they were trapped here, unable to move, the force that must already have crossed the river in pursuit of them would close the net ever tighter to their rear. At last the helicopter, maintaining its pattern of search, disappeared from view over the ridge above; but the sound of its blades came back, cutting and vicious, a probable companion for the rest of the day. MacConnachie rose at once.

'Let's get on, for God's sake! We've lost an hour!'

He tried to increase their pace, but the terrain wouldn't co-operate. Beyond a certain point, their boots found no purchase in the scrub: they fell into an angry, flurried labour up the scarp. All the time the sounds of the helicopter tormented them, suddenly increasing in volume so that they thought it had turned back, and then diminishing as they unlocked painfully from the conditioned stillness into which they had frozen. At one point, MacConnachie lost his grip on the suitcase, and it was only by chance that it fell at the feet of Ansell who, without looking, trapped it automatically. Otherwise, they would have had the entire feature to climb again.

Thirty feet below the crest, the angle of ascent increased so drastically that they were forced to crawl. By the time they reached the summit, they were hot, dirty and exhausted, and had lost even more time.

MacConnachie had been right. This was the first of two main spinal ridges. The second lay directly ahead, right across their front, fifteen to twenty miles away.

Between the two was a wasteland of smaller hills, scarps, gullies, shelves and scrub. This was the first area of maximum danger. During the next twenty-four hours, the odds would always favour recapture rather than escape.

The helicopter was about a mile ahead, below their present height, continuing to execute its neat, untiring patterns. Ansell said, reaching for breath,

'Shall we take a chance and keep moving?'

'We've got to. How well can they see out the back of those things?'

'Not well. It's an early model. Boxed-in. They have to stick their heads out to look back.'

'They won't do much of that. Let's move.'

The first stretch was downhill to a gully. As he led the way, MacConnachie called back over his shoulder,

'You see the main ridge on the horizon?'

'Yes.'

'There's a secondary height, two thirds of the way there. Got that?'

'It's got two pimples on the top.'

'That's the one. Well, that's our objective for today.'

'Oh,' said Ansell. 'Right.'

It looked a hell of a long way.

For three hours they laboured in silence, following in the wake of the dancing aircraft, crossing gullies, ascending slopes, descending them with greater care for they were then exposed, always trying to maintain an all-round watch and an even pace. The sun rose steadily to its height, and the heat grew more oppressive; sweat ran from them without pause. The suspicion grew in MacConnachie's mind that they had been spotted.

Although the helicopter never altered its intricate pattern, gradually drawing farther away from them, something about its disposition caused him to feel, with increasing certainty, that they were being trailed from in front.

A well-trained soldier would consider no other course of action. To turn back would be to warn them; to stay in formation and talk the infantry in by radio might well be to deceive them.

After five more minutes, MacConnachie could ignore his instinct no longer. They had to act. The sense of a trap jangled all around him.

The moment they descended into ground dead to the aircraft, behind a slight rise, he called,

'Go right.'

'What's up?'

'I think we've been spotted.'

They ran, crouching low, along to their right, keeping behind the rise. After two hundred yards they came to a gully into which they dropped. By working their way along it through the scrub

43

tangled in its floor, they were able to emerge behind a second feature higher than the first. Hauling themselves out, they wormed their way to the top.

'He's still in formation,' said Ansell. 'Where does that get us?'

'Wait and see.'

But in the next fifteen minutes, the helicopter made no deviation whatever from its pre-set pattern. MacConnachie swore.

'Christ! He's better than I thought.'

'He may not have seen us.'

'That's the trouble, we don't know.'

Again they waited, but nothing happened. Ansell said,

'So what do we do?'

MacConnachie scowled in frustration.

'We stay in dead ground.'

'We'll lose a lot of time.'

'We haven't any choice. If he did spot us, he's lost us now. Let's keep it that way.'

'But if he did spot us, the Goons will be coming up behind like the clappers.'

'I know that!' shouted MacConnachie, suddenly furious.

They were both tired, and badly in need of their midday break, but they kept going, always in the worst conditions, driven once more into the low ground that they hated, floundering on, struggling up gullies, creeping from dip to dip, for ever searching ahead for the next patch of dead ground. At times they were forced to detour by as much as four hundred yards, but never once did the helicopter make any move to come after them. At last, sweaty and maddened, MacConnachie halted.

'He's not *that* good, for Christ's sake!'

But Ansell said nothing, watching MacConnachie struggle with years of training that told him to move on, not to stop, to get into higher ground before he rested. At length, gracelessly, MacConnachie said,

'Five minutes. But keep watch! We won't drink yet, we'll see if we need it at the end of the rest.'

Ansell sat opposite him, and closed his eyes. Then he heard MacConnachie say, 'Here, take a pull at this,' and felt the neck of the canteen at his mouth, and then the water splashing sharply into his throat. He gulped quickly and pushed the canteen away.

'Um. Fine. Fine.'

MacConnachie screwed the stopper back on. Ansell said,

'Have yours.'

'I have. You were half asleep.'

Ansell didn't know whether he lied or told the truth, but he felt better. He got up quickly to demonstrate his fitness, making a great display of jerking his limbs into life, saying briskly,

'We'd better get going again.'

MacConnachie chuckled.

'You won't rest, will you, kid?'

'I'm a slave-driver.'

But Ansell was cross at his own weakness, and MacConnachie's easy acceptance of it. When MacConnachie rose with much simulated resignation, Ansell could have kicked him. Then the buzz of the helicopter's rotor changed in tone.

'He's coming back!'

They fell to the ground and lay still. Having taken such pains to keep out of its sight, they were now equally unable to see it, but, to judge from the sound, it was going away from them and not towards them. At length, when the swishing had died to a whisper, MacConnachie muttered, 'I'm going to see,' and wriggled away to the nearest high ground. Ansell waited. When the sound had entirely stopped, MacConnachie returned, walking upright once more.

'He's gone.'

'Refuelling?'

'I don't know. Would they need to refuel so soon?'

'I don't know.'

MacConnachie scowled.

'We still don't know whether he spotted us or not.'

'Mac, I think you were right. I think he did.'

'So do I.'

There was a silence, then MacConnachie said,

'Well, he doesn't know where we are now. Let's move.'

But he did. They had gone ten yards when Ansell knew
something was terribly wrong; and just before it happened, he
knew what it was. He screamed out, 'Mac! The chopper!'

Then a vast, tumultuous swishing closed suddenly over them
as the helicopter came in low, sneak-hitting from behind, less
than twenty feet above the ground. They were caught without
warning in a rushing maelstrom of dust and swirling air and a
great beating of sound, and then the machine was past and turning to come back. MacConnachie shouted, 'Right! Go right!'

Ansell saw him run, crouching, full tilt in that direction. He
put his head down and followed, stretching his aching legs to
their limit, struggling not to be left too far behind. The canteen
crashed repeatedly against his right thigh.

The helicopter had turned along their new path of flight and
now came roaring down on them again. MacConnachie shouted,
'Left!' and as they changed direction the chopper came about with
them, sucking them once more into the roaring vortex of sound
and heated air. The whole earth seemed to buck and tilt under
the great black shadows of the sweeping blades and Ansell,
stunned by the sheer, monstrous weight of the thing, skittered
about, losing his sense of direction.

MacConnachie had broken again to a flank and Ansell went
after him, skidding down a narrow defile between two low hills,
almost crying out with relief as they escaped the clamorous din
and raging wind. This was a terror operation, designed to intimi-
date and panic them.

They had a tighter turning-circle than the aircraft and Mac-

Connachie jinked again, cutting out a new angle of flight, Ansell at his heels. But the pilot knew his job. After each swoop he pulled up to enlarge his field of vision, giving them no chance to cut back and slip him. As he bore down again, MacConnachie broke right, and he and Ansell ran under the aircraft, bullocking their way through the gauntlet of driven air and buffeting sound, breaking then to their right again and running headlong for a gully out to the side of the two hills, where they threw themselves into the undergrowth as the engine roared and the pilot fought to bring his machine hard about.

They were both gasping for breath, heaving and straining, but MacConnachie pushed Ansell brutally along the gully, shouting above the clamour of the engine,

'Move! Move!'

'Can't we shoot it down?'

'No! Move!'

Ansell scrabbled and floundered through the scrub, trying to escape up the gully, moaning for air, but the helicopter gained height rapidly, pulling back in a wide circle. There was no over-hang to hide them, and as soon as they could see the aircraft, they knew the pilot could see them.

They broke from cover once more, scrambling out of the gully and back to the two hills, where they ran down the defile again from the other end, as the helicopter beat over them, momentarily darkening the sun with its flashing arc of steel. Ansell crashed into MacConnachie, as MacConnachie stopped abruptly.

'Shoot it, Mac!'

'Not yet! Double back! Move!'

Ansell was pitched violently into a stumbling run as Mac-Connachie thrust him off, then sensed rather than heard Mac-Connachie thudding after him as he ran under the aircraft and back up the defile for the third time. He was almost done. His heart churned and leaped in his rib-cage, terrifying him with the force of its palpitations. He could hardly draw breath. There was no lack of will, but a failure of his body to match MacConnachie's. Coming out of the defile, he fell. MacConnachie's boot crunched into his side, which may have been an accident, and MacConnachie raged, 'Get up! Get up!'

But Ansell couldn't. He was seized by the left shoulder and dragged round the end of one of the hills, just long enough to get his legs functioning again. MacConnachie was leading them back the way they had come, but this time he was going round the hill instead of along the defile; by the time they had reached its entrance yet again, Ansell was managing to progress under his own power, and the crisis was passing. MacConnachie pressed him down against the side of the hill and shouted in his ear,

'Where's the petrol tank on that thing?'

'What?'

'The tank—where is it?'

'Round the back—behind the cabin. You can't hit it from below.'

The engine was roaring as the pilot pulled the chopper up and round for another sweep. But, despite his condition, Ansell could tell that it was headed for the wrong end of the defile, momentarily out of contact with them, and he realized that this must have been MacConnachie's intention. MacConnachie shouted,

'I'll have to get him from the side. I've got to kill him with the first shot, or he'll go up out of range.'

Ansell could see now that MacConnachie was grey-faced, drawn, and labouring for breath as badly as himself. But the thirty seconds MacConnachie had won were invaluable. With a returning sense of anguish and fury, Ansell looked up at the sky.

'What the bloody hell's he playing at, anyway?'

'He's showing off!'

'*What?*'

'Showing off!'

And then MacConnachie's expression broke into one of amused appreciation, and he shook with laughter. Still laughing, he said,

'Oh God, the clever bastard! He's coming up this side!'

The helicopter slid in towards them once more, low against the side of the hill. They were up and off, headlong down the defile for the fourth time. It seemed to Ansell that in some horrible way the proportions of their world had been reversed: the tiny speck of dancing metal had swollen to immense, crushing dimensions; they had been reduced to minute, scrabbling dwarfs on an endless landscape. The hide-and-seek went on, destructive and inescapable: out of the defile, across to the gully, back, and along the defile again; and always the pilot was clever enough to judge their pace, guess their direction, and peg them tight. They were being run into the ground.

Once more, when they had slipped the aircraft for a few seconds, they lay against the hillside, panting.

'No good! Can't lose him. Got to bring him in just right.'

'What do I do?'

'Run for the pimple. See it?'

Following the direction of MacConnachie's trembling arm, Ansell saw the feature he was indicating.

'Yes.'

'Get there! Wait!' MacConnachie swallowed convulsively. 'When the chopper comes—run back—across my front. I'll be here. Right?'

MacConnachie gripped Ansell's arm, waiting for the moment to send him off. Ansell steeled himself to run two hundred yards; it seemed an impossible task. The helicopter thrashed in from their right.

'Go!'

Ansell ran blindly, with a shocking absence of co-ordination, pitching and staggering over the pitted earth. He seemed hardly to be moving at all, scarcely to grow any closer to his objective from one frenzied glimpse to the next. The more he tried to drive his legs on, the weaker they became. He was on the point of giving up when he ran into the pimple, and lay against it, whimpering. After some moments, he dragged himself round it, to lie hidden from the helicopter.

As soon as Ansell left him, MacConnachie felt stronger, lighter, refreshed by an access of power and confidence. Alone, he could take that chopper. He didn't need Ansell.

As the helicopter bore in, he slipped round the hill and down the defile, leaving the suitcase at his firing point. The moment he heard the pilot pull up to cross the twin hills, he skidded about and ran back, leaving the defile from the same end, laughing.

I've got you. At last I've got you cold, you bastard, and you know it.

MacConnachie could hear the pilot's fury in the roar of the engine as, blind for the first time, he fought to heave his machine tight about. In those seconds of dead visibility, MacConnachie ran across and down into the gully.

Now what are you going to do, bastard? You've got to traverse the defile and the hills first; thirty wasted seconds. Then you've got to get up and round to sweep the gully, and as you run dead off the hills, I'll get back among them again. That's another wasted circuit. Then when you come back to the hills, you've got to go left or right; and whichever you choose, I'll choose the other. You're cobblered, my friend. You won't catch me in this lot. And comes the time you have to go after Ansell, I've got you.

Exactly as MacConnachie predicted, the helicopter flew its course. By the time he was back in the hills, the pilot was over the gully, and MacConnachie knew he was worried. It would have been strictly against orders to buzz them, but he needed contact with the enemy, this man, he needed the release that comes from pursuit and kill. MacConnachie knew him as he knew himself, and this made him strong.

Oh, but he was a clever bastard, though. He made his run to the left of the hills coming off the gully, then, halfway up, crossed over to the right. MacConnachie had seen it coming and, laughing with appreciation, he readjusted his own position to maintain a dead location. Everything the man did appealed to him, satisfied his sense of tactical rightness. The tighter the conflict became, the more MacConnachie's admiration for his adversary grew.

Now the pilot pulled out to go after Ansell, but MacConnachie sat tight, grinning. Sure enough, the manoeuvre turned into a hard about-face, and the man came roaring back for one last very low run across the hills. MacConnachie applauded with delight.

This time, he knew, the pilot had gone in earnest, committing himself to the attempt to locate Ansell. He moved quickly to his prearranged firing position. The question was, could Ansell lure that man, under pressure, to leave himself open long enough for just one shot? Throughout the entire battle so far, with all its manoeuvrings, the pilot had not given him one clear look at the tank; his skill was prodigious. If he made a mistake now, it would be just the one. There would be no second chance. The man was too good for that.

So was MacConnachie.

At first Ansell had lain, with a sudden and terrible sense of isolation, watching the helicopter swoop back and forth across the hills, wracked by his inability to intervene, his legs jerking and clenching with every twist of MacConnachie's flight, as he imagined it to be. Then, free for the moment of MacConnachie's bullying, he had started to think. The plan could be improved.

To run the chopper on to MacConnachie's gun was simple and direct, just the sort of improvisation he would expect of

MacConnachie. But if he moved *now* to a flank, he could lead the helicopter in *across* MacConnachie's field of fire and, by angling towards MacConnachie at the right moment, cause it also to dip, thus exposing what might prove to be the vital extra inches of tank. He was convinced also that if the aircraft found him already out to one flank, it would be more likely to follow the path he cut out.

First, he rid himself of the canteen, burying it deeply in a crack near the pimple, and covering it with hastily yanked handfuls of scrub. The observer in the helicopter would be armed and, given a chance at the unprotected canteen, could deprive them of water and reduce their fighting effectiveness by ninety per cent at a single stroke.

Then he selected his route, and slipped away.

MacConnachie was furious and baffled. The helicopter had reached the pimple and clearly had not sighted Ansell. It began to search in wider and wider arcs of flight.

'What are you playing at, you stupid little bastard?'

But nothing happened, and MacConnachie raged. Had he seen Ansell's manoeuvre, he would have admired it. But had he looked, he would not have seen it; light made little difference to Ansell's gift of invisibility.

'Oh, goddammit, run—run!'

It suddenly dawned on Ansell that he was clean away. He had only to keep going, and they would never find him. But it wasn't true, he knew. He was free now because MacConnachie had freed him. Once it got tough again, he would need MacConnachie's blundering resolution to save him. All the same, he felt an enormous flush of satisfaction.

As soon as the chopper came near, he showed himself. He ran a little to the left, stumbled, turned back and ran to the right. When he was sure he had created a convincing impression of panic, he set out across MacConnachie's front, aiming for a point between MacConnachie's firing position on his left and the pimple on his right. Without the canteen, he ran much more easily.

'Oh, you clever little perisher,' murmured MacConnachie, chuckling, 'you fly bastard.'

He brought the gun up and checked the sights. Less than two hundred yards, open-sight firing. That meant three snap shots, close together, correcting on each shot. Four seconds shooting, one chopper to bag. You're joking, of course.

Ansell was going like the clappers, stretching out like a lover with a shot-gun up his tail. No canteen. Check that after. The helicopter came round, falling in behind him.

MacConnachie was sure the pilot would be raging by now, determined to buzz Ansell savagely. There was no doubt he was coming in far too low. Carelessly low. Beautifully low.

MacConnachie held the gun gently until it was part of him, taking a long, slow breath. Fifty yards to come.

Ansell was tiring rapidly, gulping air, driving himself to maintain pace. His cheeks seemed to have swollen to the size of balloons, and as he bounced up and down they flapped in and out of his lower field of vision like white dewlaps of blubber. The demoralizing illusion came to him again that he was getting nowhere, and the terror, far from being pretended, was now real. The chopper was low. Too low. It was going to hit him. The swishing, chilling whine paralysed him. He was going to be hit. Hit. There's the pimple. Go left. Turn. Stumble. Ankles crack together. Stay upright. Stay upright.

Perfect. Coming in just right. The kid still fifteen feet ahead, not flagging. He'll have to go like the devil when that thing explodes.

Vaguely aware somebody leaning out of the cab. Must be the observer. Pilot on the other side. Could get a shot in now. Wait. Wait.

Breaking in towards me. Lovely. Well done. Here comes the chopper. Dip, you bastard. Dip. That's better. Bit more. Bit more ...

Where's the tank, then? Where's the bloody tank, for Christ's sake?

Doesn't matter! Shoot it high, in the neck, just behind the head.

MacConnachie rose, stepped out, whipped up the gun, and took aim down the narrow corridor below the flashing blades of steel.

Then he saw Ansell was down.

Get up. In God's name, get up!

Ansell had crashed down with such force that he was winded. He had no idea what was happening. The roaring, swishing horror closed over him.

Doesn't matter. Take a chance. Shoot.

And then ...

Oh, no. Oh, sweet Jesus, no. He's shooting at him. The bloody man's leaning out of the cab and he's shooting at the boy. Ludicrously, MacConnachie took another step forward, protesting at this breach of orders.

'That's not right! It can't be!'

Then he aimed at the head, and put in three shots, tight and neat. The figure slumped, and the gun tumbled down like a twig in a high wind.

Realign. Too late. Too late.

He got off two shots, but missed by a mile as the helicopter swept up, gaining altitude rapidly. Furious and frustrated, he took careful aim at the perspex frontage, and fired three more

spaced shots. But he was wasting his time. On the side blind to
the pilot, and at this range, he might just as well throw stones.

Ansell was staggering up, holding his head. MacConnachie
ran to him.

Ansell shouted,
'What happened?'
'I missed.'
'You *what*?'
'Are you all right?'
'You *missed*?'
'Yes.'
'You stupid bastard!'
MacConnachie ran to the fallen gun and picked it up.
'Take this!'
'Where the hell did that come from?'
'Come on!'
MacConnachie ran back to the hill. Ansell screamed after him,
'You stupid bastard!'

They had achieved nothing but to exhaust themselves. The
helicopter sat above, comfortably out of range, waiting. They
sat below, not bothering to hide. It was a grotesque situation, and
bitterness wriggled between them like worms.
'How the hell did you come to miss him?'
'It wasn't an easy lay, you know!'
'I brought him in just right—I know I did!'
'And you fell!'
'I wasn't in your bloody light, was I?'
'He was shooting at you!'
'Who was?'
'The observer!'
'So?'
'I saved your life!'

'It was your job to kill that thing, not look after me!'

'You ungrateful bastard!'

'What am I supposed to be grateful for—another gun? Next time, for Christ's sake do what you plan to do!'

'Get stuffed!'

MacConnachie stamped off and churned about in the scrub, muttering angrily,

'How the hell did I get lumbered with you in the first place?'

'You chose me. I was no friend.'

'You aren't now!'

'All right, then—let's go our own ways!'

'Let's do that!'

A silence. Ansell said,

'If we can't trust one another, we might just as well.'

MacConnachie said,

'I didn't see any tank, I'll tell you that. There was damn-all tank on the back of that thing.'

'What did you expect it to be? Painted bright red and labelled petrol?'

'Now, look, kid—'

'No, you look! I told you where it is—now trust me. We trust one another, or we've had it! I rely on you, bloody well rely on me!'

MacConnachie turned away, and after a moment said quietly,

'I do rely on you.'

'All right, trust me then. We can't afford another mistake like that.'

'All right, all right! We were both wrong. Now forget it!'

Ansell had to settle for that. He reached for their new gun, and began to strip it down. MacConnachie said,

'I'll do it.'

But Ansell ignored him. *Trust*. MacConnachie sat at his side and looked up at the helicopter.

'We've got him for the rest of the day.'

'Um. It's funny.'

'I'm glad somebody thinks so.'

'I mean, he can't come down in case we hit him. But we don't want to use ammunition. So he sits there, and we sit here, and neither of us does anything but watch the other.'

'He's doing something. He's talking in the Goons right now. We'll have to move soon.'

Ansell had unscrewed the barrel of the gun; he sighted along it, then handed it to MacConnachie. It was impossible to see from one end through to the other. The gun had struck barrel down, damaging that component beyond repair. MacConnachie said,

'Great for shooting round corners.'

'That's what I thought. The rest of it's okay, though.'

'What about the magazine?'

'Nearly full.'

'We'll keep that and the breech-block when we chuck it away. Hang on to it for now.'

'Right.'

Concentrating on reassembling the weapon, Ansell said carefully,

'Was he really trying to kill me, do you think? That'd be against orders; they'll take us alive, if they can.'

MacConnachie flushed.

'Can't think of everything, you go by instinct.'

'I mean, he must be pretty clever, to have someone leaning out of the cab, just in case you took a shot at him.'

MacConnachie glared up at the sky.

'He's clever,' he muttered, 'that man, he's good.'

The kid was right. He should have gone for the chopper. He shouldn't have been fooled. But what the hell did he expect? Sackcloth and ashes. Counter-attack.

'Where the hell's the canteen?'

'Behind the pimple.'

'Is it hidden?'

'Of course.'

'Are you sure?'

'Yes.'

'Well, are you?'

'I don't make mistakes like that.'

It wasn't the mistake Ansell would have expected of Mac-Connachie. A too great ruthlessness, yes; a careless overplaying of the hand. But an absence of ruthlessness, that was disturbing. To see MacConnachie unsettled, as now, was to suffer a frightening lapse in his own confidence. He needed MacConnachie, stupid, fearless and bold. Without him, he could never survive; and for that, he should be prepared to pay any price. He looked at the sulking figure, and smiled with affection. Not stupid, limited. He said,

'I'm sorry, Mac. I'll bet you got him.'

'Of course. Three times. They all struck.'

'Will the pilot go back for that?'

'Not him. If the observer's dead, it doesn't matter. If he's still alive, that man will let him bleed to death. It's what I'd do.' MacConnachie screwed up his eyes as though projecting himself into the helicopter. 'There's brains all over the inside of that crate.'

'Nasty.'

'He's not bothered. He wants us now, so bad.' MacConnachie's voice was as soft as Ansell had heard it. 'He'll stick till his petrol runs out.'

'Soon?'

MacConnachie slowly unlocked his eyes from the helicopter to look back at the last ridge.

'Not soon enough. The River Boys are very close now. We'll move.'

Ansell rose with the reassembled gun; MacConnachie took up the undamaged weapon and the suitcase. Ansell said,

'Where are the other choppers?'

'Don't be greedy.' Then MacConnachie looked up at the helicopter, waved his gun towards the distant heights, and shouted,

'Oi! We're going that-a-way!'

Ansell was sure the pilot waved back.

From the pimple, where they retrieved the canteen, they headed for the secondary height, their day's objective. Already it was afternoon, and the sun was falling towards the horizon. They were badly behind schedule, and had no chance of completing the planned march by nightfall. Ansell said,

'Is there any point in leading the chopper the wrong way?'

'No. We have to cross the ridge. They'll cover the whole thing.'

And so the helicopter came with them, never far ahead, never far behind, an unshakeable and unmistakable marker as to their location. In a curious way, thought Ansell, they were not ungrateful for his company.

The sun lay low, the shadows stretched eerily, and Ansell was tired: for the first time, really weary, dragging himself along. Hill followed hill, gully joined gully behind them, each indistinguishable from the last, or the next. He was at a low ebb, knees aching and ankles unreliable. But, in a daze, he maintained his all-round watch: right and to the rear, left and to the rear, then fully behind. He wondered how much longer he would stay awake.

MacConnachie had been staring at, and through, the country ahead, reaching beyond the heights for each protuberance, shelf and configuration. He had them now. He knew them.

They could march by night.

The two things happened almost together.

First, the helicopter left them, turning back to disappear over the sun-bright ridge behind, giving one last wink of its blades in the dying sun. Sudden quiet. Then Ansell saw, or thought he saw, movement on the ridge.

'Mac.'

'What?'

'I think the River Boys are with us.'

From the comparative darkness of the plain, they could see the still glowing forward slopes of the ridge clearly. Tiny figures appeared on the skyline, forerunners of a larger party.

'It was bound to happen.'

'They can't see us.'

'They know where we are. That's why our friend could retire for the night.'

MacConnachie turned forward again to look up at their target feature for the day. He said,

'We're four hours from the top of that thing. We'll get up there, and then decide what to do.'

Ansell nodded wearily.

As they climbed, night overtook them, reaching the summit long before they did. It grew cold, and very dark. Later, perhaps, the translucent glow of the previous night might reappear, but in these first hours there was nothing to warn them of the ankle-wrenching pothole or the foot-snaring cranny. Tedium flowered into every kind of small agony, until their nerves contracted at each jar, and their systems cried out in disproportion for relief. A major catastrophe might have spurred them to greater effort; a shower of rain could have unmanned them completely.

The ascent took six hours, and when they reached the peak, near midnight, the sky grew light too late to help them.

'Oh God.' Ansell lay back with his eyes shut. 'I'm so tired.
'Me too.'
Silence.
'What now?'
'It'll take them eight hours to reach us.'
'They won't come tonight.'
'They've got to. They know where we are, they know we're tired. They won't get so good a chance again.'
'They must be tired too.'
'Not as tired as we are. They're hunting, we're running.
'Now I know how the animals feel.'
'That's something in your favour.'
Silence.
'So what do we do?'
'Sleep. Four hours. That'll leave us well ahead. If we don't sleep, we go nowhere.'
'Good. Give me the gun.'
'What?'
Ansell took the gun, fiddled with it, and pushed it back to MacConnachie.
'It's still on single-shot. Good night.'
He rolled over to sleep. MacConnachie chuckled.
'Food first.'
'You're joking.'
'We eat, then we sleep.'
'Oh, come on.'
'Do what you're bloody well told!'
Ansell sat up, muttering mutinously, while MacConnachie unroped the suitcase in the darkness and opened it.
'I don't see what the bloody hell...'
'Shut up!'
MacConnachie was groping about in the suitcase, trying to identify one tin against another in the pale light. He suddenly said,

'What order are they in?'

'What order are what in?'

'The *tins*, for Christ's sake!'

'What do you mean, order?'

'Well, you put 'em in order, didn't you? How do we tell one from another at night—strike a bloody match?'

'Are you taking the mickey?'

'You stupid little bastard—don't you think of the simplest things?'

'What does it matter?'

'It matters whether we have hot soup or cold soup; when we can light a fire, and when we can't!'

'I'm not hungry anyway!'

'You'll bloody well eat when I tell you!'

Both men lost their anger simultaneously. After a moment, Ansell murmured,

'You can tell them apart by feeling their bottoms.'

'It's their contents I'm interested in, not their sex.'

'For God's sake, look!' Ansell rummaged in the case. 'The big one's condensed milk. That's that one. The soup have got rings round the bottom. The meat haven't. That's meat.'

'Why the hell didn't you say so?'

'I didn't think of it.'

'Well done.'

MacConnachie tore open the tin with a knife, and gouged out a hunk of meat for Ansell.

'Half now, half before we set out.'

'Thanks.'

MacConnachie then cut out his own piece, and they sat eating. Ansell said,

'It's pretty nauseating.'

'Be grateful.'

'I am.'

They had a drink each, and slept; but not before, at Macconnachie's insistence, they had untied their slacks from round their waists, put them on, and then their uniform jackets. This last function MacConnachie had to perform for Ansell, who slept on his feet like a scratchily exhausted infant.

Under the blanket, they huddled together for warmth.

It seemed to Ansell that he had barely lost consciousness when, four hours later, MacConnachie was pulling off the blanket and shaking him.

'Time to move.'

'God, oh God.'

Exhaustion lay over him like a sheet of lead. He struggled to come awake as a man buried under a collapsed building struggles, hopelessly against impossible odds. MacConnachie shook him more brutally.

'Wake up, damn you!'

His head rattled about, his half-formed thoughts careened, as MacConnachie gripped his coat front and wrenched him violently back and forth. When MacConnachie let go, he put a hand to his head, and muttered,

' 'm tired.'

'So am I!'

Then MacConnachie struck him across the face, knocking his arm aside.

'Wake up, you gutless little bastard!'

Ansell woke.

'Sorry.'

'That's better,' said MacConnachie, and turned away. Ansell felt suddenly very sick but, although he retched, nothing came, and it passed almost at once.

'Morning sickness,' he said. MacConnachie said,
'Get changed and ready to move.'

MacConnachie was busy in the gloom, stripping off his jacket, packing it with the blanket, tying his slacks round his waist again. Ansell said,

'It won't happen again.'

'It'll be my turn to lie in tomorrow.'

As they worked, preparing for the new day's march, Ansell came to understand their physical condition. It was now 'the day after tomorrow', the moment at which the effect of their initial outlay of effort should overtake them, and it did. He ached at every joint; each limb flared in pain at the smallest movement. His stomach was unnaturally tender, his neck and shoulder muscles cracked audibly, and every time he stooped his head spun. But the greatest pain came from his feet, which were badly blistered, and his left shoulder, which had been eroded by the strap of the canteen and burned persistently. All the same, he knew that MacConnachie was no better off than himself; and if MacConnachie didn't complain, he wasn't going to.

As if reading his thoughts, MacConnachie laughed and said,

'It'll go.'

'It had better.

MacConnachie packed the empty tin and the second breech-block, roped up the case, and thrust the remains of the damaged gun deep into a fissure, where it should lie hidden for ever; the spare magazine was already under his belt. The meat he had scooped on to a little pile of grass, and now they had breakfast, and then a drink. Finally, MacConnachie scratched a shallow hole in the earth but, apart from urinating, it was a forlorn hope for them both.

'It'll come.'

They advanced to peer down into the gloom.

'Damn. We'll be in low ground when the sun comes up.

'At least they won't see us.'

'They will when the chopper comes.'

The back slope of the secondary feature proved unexpectedly steep, and they fell many times in the half-light, jarring their bodies painfully. But as the descent unwound, Ansell came slowly to realize that each new impact, with the effort of concentration to which it gave rise, was driving the aching stiffness from his bones, routing the over-sensitivity from cringing nerves. A small victory was being won, and it gave him renewed zest. They would never set out so tired again.

MacConnachie was concerned. Day had broken in the high ground above, but still they travelled downhill, enveloped now in a thick mist that had risen, pale and mysterious, with the dawn. Somewhere ahead the bulk of the main ridge loomed, but he was blind.

Then, as gently as it had come, the mist melted away, and the massif stood before them, two hundred yards to their front. A towering, scrub-grown scar rose straight up its sheer face, much like the one they had climbed the day before, but infinitely taller. It was the only available cover and, now that they were exposed to the sky, he led the way hurriedly towards it, humping over cracks and gullies, taking many anxious glances over his shoulder for the helicopter.

At the foot of the scar, he crouched and waited for Ansell.

'We're going up that. Stay close, but not less than ten feet. When the chopper comes, close up to talk.'

'Right.'

'And stop grinning all the time.'

'I'm happy in my work.'

Ansell didn't grin for long. The scrub was, if anything, even thicker than the day before, twisted and tough, gnarled and deep-rooted. Certainly the slope was steeper. Every yard had to be fought for and won; nothing was yielded; and the cost was measured in torn fingers, wrenched ankles, and nails laid back. He came to feel tiny again, in face of an impossible ascent. Sheer, repetitious labour took command.

Then the helicopter came, and they burrowed deep into the brush.

Ansell started to worm his way upwards through the binding growth, heading for the point at which he had last glimpsed MacConnachie, but somehow, with the dust puffing in his face, and the chopper swishing rapidly closer, he missed him. He rooted about with the beginnings of panic. Then MacConnachie called, 'Here, here!' and he turned left, wriggling towards the voice. From the height of a small animal's head, it was impossible to see beyond the nearest stalks, and it was without warning that he came up suddenly against MacConnachie's back. MacConnachie hissed, 'Still! Lie still!'

The helicopter seemed to be almost directly overhead, its blades beating the air about them, the scrub rustling furiously in the buffeting down-draught. He didn't want to risk exposing his face, so he shouted into the ground,

'Has he spotted us?'

'No.'

It was becoming oppressively hot again as the sun marched up the sky. Heat not only beat down on their unprotected heads and backs, but rose up into their faces in stifling waves from the earth. To gain some relief, Ansell very slowly raised his head a little until he could look back at the secondary feature; he saw to his disappointment that they were still below the level of the peak where they had spent the night; they had travelled no more than two hundred feet up the scarp. Sweat ran into his eyes and curled under his chin to hang there, tickling. He lowered his face again and listened to the helicopter as it moved off, the sound rising and falling, marking the pattern of the search they would have to avoid. After a while, MacConnachie said,

'God, this is a bastard. He's doing a lateral search, sweeping half a mile in each direction, working his way up the scar.'

'What do we do?'

'Only one thing. Crawl when he's at the end of the sweep, freeze when he comes close again.'

'But that'll take hours! Days!'

'I know it.' Then, urgently, 'Watch it! Keep still!'

The chopper swept in over their position again, hovered, and slid back the way it had come. As the rotors diminished, MacConnachie said,

'He's got to change his pattern sometime. Till he does, we're lumbered.'

'But we'll never get away like this!'

'We'll never get away if we're seen.'

The next hour was one of grinding, remorseless agony: a succession of frantic bursts, too hurried to make anything like optimum progress, interspersed with periods of wracking doubt as, the helicopter once more beating overhead, they lay in rigid, sweating stillness, wondering if their too-hastily-adopted positions were apparent from above. But never long to wonder, for they would be off again, driving their faces through the tearing brush, gulping mouthfuls of dust-thick air, never escaping from the closeness of the baked earth. This was, for Ansell, the most destructive factor of all: never to be able to lift his face from the dirt; to be for ever locked in the ignoble posture of panic. He longed to rise from the stifling confinement, to escape the abject acceptance of their position and the gasping contortions of a beached fish.

Not one of their breaks carried them farther than twenty feet up the scarp; most, less; and by the time the helicopter had reached the peak, and turned off to return to the foot of the ridge, they had travelled no more than another hundred feet up the height. In an agony of discomfort, they watched as the pilot snouted about, setting up another pattern of search.

'Go left,' MacConnachie pleaded; 'go out to the side, you bastard.'

But the helicopter settled on a pattern which took the scar itself for a centre, and they knew they were desperately placed.

It was the same man. It had to be. That man would *know*, he would not need to be told, that MacConnachie and Ansell were in the scarp. There was nowhere else they could be. It was where, in their position, he would be.

Hating him, admiring him, MacConnachie waited, nagged by the need to go on, watching for the moment to launch himself forward again.

Above all things he hated this: doing nothing.

The punishment continued: an unremitting compound of flustered, ineffective activity and confined, tormenting heat. All the while their precious store of time fled them, and their hearts ached. There seemed no escape: just a slow, persistent draining of their reserve. Ansell knew the tears ran down his cheeks, and he lived in terror of losing his grip on the knife.

At length the helicopter reached the peak for the second time, but it turned, and came back, and started the same pattern of search all over again.

'Oh God, oh God, it's hopeless, Mac.'

'No, kid! That's what he wants you to say.'

'It's true.'

'No!'

'It's true!'

'No! No! He'll not win! He'll *not*!'

But the chopper ground back and forth over their heads, beating the message down, that he knew where they were, that he would never go away, that he would stay and stay until they were broken into the earth.

You'll never beat us, you Goon shit, do you hear? Never. We'll win in the end. We'll break you. We'll win.

'Where are the other choppers?'
'With him up there, they don't need any others.'
'What about the River Boys?'
'It took us a day to reach the last height, it'll take them half a day at least.'
'They're not hiding!'
'They're soldiers, they won't flog themselves.'
Ansell stared at the knotted roots a few inches from his face.
'Mac,' he said, 'we might have to crawl all the way.'
'We might. If we have to, we will.'
Ansell had feared nothing more in his life. MacConnachie said, 'But we won't. He'll be gone by then.'

He wasn't.
As the sun progressed steadily up the sky to its most fierce height, the unrelenting search went on. No moment of relief, such as had come on the previous days, lifted the pressure from them. The suffocating torture was endless. First their finger-nails went, shredded and torn away, to leave their fingers bleeding stumps. The blood mingled with sweat and dirt to add one more sharp rawness to an already proliferating pain. And their cheeks flowered in a cross-work of multiplying scratches. Their arms and legs began to feel insecure in their sockets, as though stretched beyond their capacity to maintain contact, and necks and shoulders locked in a posture, almost comic, of strained watchfulness. To move at all had begun to demand a quality of will from the stomach that Ansell could feel flowing from him, useless, like spilled fuel.

At midday they reached a point level with the height on which they had spent the night, and crawled on.

Ansell's body slithered in a sickly smell of sweat. His eyes, sightless now, ran with tears. There was no air that wasn't excoriatingly hot and packed with a fine powder of dust. And all the time the helicopter flitted about with such dainty ease, with so little effort in the clean air, never quite leaving their field of vision, never allowing a moment of respite to rise and ease their wracked bodies.

There comes a moment when the body rejects pain and unconsciousness supervenes. Ansell prayed for it, but instead every nerve and tissue seemed only to become more agonizingly sensitive to the scraping jar of their journey. If only they could get up, if they could only rid themselves of the terrible anchor of the earth, which held them back with such vast competence. To tackle the slope in the least effective manner outraged his mind and heart, and rifled his store of courage.

Conviction rises in torment from the stomach until it overwhelms reason. Ansell saw that they would be climbing still when only bones were left, clacking for ever through the meaningless motions of ascent. A sort of madness, he knew, had come.

MacConnachie's mind grew dim. Should they stop, drink? One moment of carelessness would destroy everything. But what *was* everything? He laid his face in the dirt and muttered through caked lips, 'Rest.'

Ansell lay still beside him.

'Drink in a minute.'

They fell asleep.

When the helicopter, scudding low, woke them, it took MacConnachie a moment or two to work out that they had only just dozed off. They had not become stiff, and the sun was still in the same position in the sky. Ansell, too, he saw, had come awake on the instant.

'It's okay. We only went for a minute.'

Ansell's pale, tortured face broke into a faint smile.

'Nothing like a good kip to set you up.'

'That's right.'

The helicopter had returned to the foot of the ridge, and now set up another of its patient, unending patterns of search, to the right and back across the scar. MacConnachie smiled; it was no holiday for that man either. Ansell said, with quiet calm,

'We're really in it, aren't we?'

'That we are.'

MacConnachie could see two possible sources of hope, both faint. That the man might run out of fuel, or that his superiors, less intuitive, might order him to search elsewhere if he continued to report no contact. But MacConnachie did not believe that the man would go, or that the Goons, keeping such a dog, would call him off.

He tried to work out how far the River Boys were behind. Not more than five hours, nor less than four, which would put them on the secondary feature by four thirty. That meant Goons, chopper and daylight all at the same time. That was bad, because he must see over the top of the crest before night came; it was the minimum intelligence requirement. He said,

'Somehow we've got to go faster.'

Ansell said,

'We can't. And we can't reach the top by nightfall.'

MacConnachie was startled, but then he said,

'So what do we do?'

Ansell said,

'When the River Boys come, why don't we lie up? As soon as it's dark, we can move *along* the ridge to the right. That way, when daylight comes, we'll be out to the side of our own line of march. It could take them days to find us, and the longer it takes, the wider they have to search. We can march all night if we have to.'

That was the thing. Planning ahead. Using the brain. No good dropping in it, then bullocking your way out like he did. Of course they didn't know where the Goons were on the other side of the ridge, but when dawn came they would still hold the high ground, and they would see the Goons before the Goons saw them. He'd have thought of it in time—at least, he'd have done it; but to think ahead, that was the trick. Not to *feel*, to think.

'We'll do it. Drink now, then move.'

'Right.'

Flat against the earth, under the persistent swish of the rotor blades, they edged the stopper out of the canteen and drank a mouthful apiece. Then they started to climb again.

It was easy to say, 'We can march all night if we have to.' The benefit of their rest stayed with them for less than a minute, then the horror clamped down over them once again. Far from replenishing their store of strength, the rest seemed only to have sharpened their appetite for pain. It came to them from every sensitive part. The weight of the afternoon sun was massive, pressing them into the earth. Each limb seemed grotesquely swollen, each source of power hopelessly diminished. Soon Ansell moved with the dull absence of an automaton, distantly aware that his face was on fire, that his throat raged with abrasive harshness, and that a rod was being passed up his spine to the base of his neck.

More and more he came to rely on MacConnachie, rising when he rose, crawling when he crawled, falling when he fell. For a time he had raged uselessly at the earth, hating it as a good soldier hates his enemy, wanting to punish it for punishing him; but now he saw only MacConnachie. Whatever coherence remained to him was directed at that man as though, by an effort of projection, he could cause that back to drag up his own body with itself. There was no helicopter, no ridge, no discomfort; just one sole point of focus, a back, broad and strong, untouched by suffering, untouchable.

And a thought that caused him aching pain: in all this time, in all this torment, MacConnachie has never once relinquished his grip on either the suitcase or the gun.

How can I ask him to carry me as well?

MacConnachie knew he would have to stop. He was no longer watching the chopper; he was falling into a rhythm, predictable and dangerous, assuming too much. His arms ached as though his hands were wrought in steel which, stretched too far, had set in an unbreakable grip. He fell against the earth like a man struck down.

Ansell crawled to MacConnachie and, laying his face against his boot, stared unseeing.

In ten hours they had travelled, as the crow flies, less than a mile. As a man crawls, they had covered eight hundred feet of the scarp, two thirds of the way to the top. But they had never once been seen, they were still out of contact.

It was MacConnachie who slept and Ansell who kept watch, dull eyes pointed at the secondary height in dim anticipation.

The helicopter was always with them.

He woke, or became aware, to see small figures milling about on the peak of the secondary feature. Already the sun was close to the horizon, and the helicopter had gone. It was this, perhaps, the sudden silence, that had brought him to himself. He shook MacConnachie's boot, and a growl came down to him.

'What?'

'They're with us again.'

'Sun's going down. They're late.'

Silence. Then MacConnachie said,

'Go to sleep. I'll wake you when it's time to move.

'Not yet?'

'Not yet.'

It was cold when MacConnachie woke him, and dark. Night had fallen. MacConnachie pushed something soft and squishy into his hand and said,

'Eat this.'

'What is it?'

'Last of the fruit from the village.'

They spoke in hushed tones, for sound travels far at night. Ansell took a mouthful of the rich flesh and crushed it against his gums to release the juices, which he swallowed, gasping,

'Phew! That's fiery stuff.'

'Saved us a tin of meat.'

'A man could get drunk on it.'

'Don't do that.'

MacConnachie checked the gun in the darkness while Ansell, continuing to eat, said,

'It's as good as a drink. We can save water, too.'

'Tonight we're having condensed milk.'

'Oh God, I hate that stuff.'

'Now the tin's open, you'll drink it. I've had mine.'

'You probably like it.'

'Nothing to do with it.'

'Not for you.'

When he had finished, Ansell sat very still, but MacConnachie noticed and, taking his hand, clamped it firmly round the tin.

'Drink!'

Ansell shut his eyes, located one of the holes with his tongue and, tilting back his head, tried to swallow it down, as a child might, without touching the sides. MacConnachie grunted with satisfaction, took back the empty tin and packed it. After a moment, Ansell said,

'Can we have a little water now?'

'What for?'

'Take the taste away.'

'For God's sake!'

'It makes me sick, Mac. It really does.'

'All right; just a little. Hurry it up!'

Ansell opened the canteen while MacConnachie, muttering, roped up the suitcase. Then Ansell said,

'Are you going to have some?'

'No, I'm all right.'

Silence.

'If you don't, I can't.'

'Christ Almighty!'

The dark shape of MacConnachie loomed up, seized the canteen, drank, and thrust it back into Ansell's arms.

'Now drink! And shut up!'

Ansell washed out his mouth and swallowed. He was much recovered from the day's ordeal and, looking about, he was struck by a sudden feeling of unease: there was something very strange about the texture of the night. Abruptly he said,

'What time is it?'

MacConnachie, as though he had been waiting for this question, hesitated before he replied.

'About midnight.'

'*Midnight?*'

'Shut up! What are you trying to do—broadcast our position?'

'But for God's sake!'

'It doesn't matter!'

'What do you mean, it... ?'

'Shut up and *listen*!'

Ansell, shocked by a sense of betrayal, clamped his mouth

shut. MacConnachie's face was close to his, their altercation carried out in fierce whispers. MacConnachie was saying,

'We needed the rest! They've got the same climb we had, but they've got to do it by night. And in a minute we'll be out to the side—they can climb till Kingdom Come, they won't find us. So don't panic, we're all right.'

Without a word, Ansell re-stoppered the canteen, rose, turned away, and hitched the strap over his right shoulder, where it had rubbed all day. The left still burned painfully from the day before. MacConnachie swore, and assumed his own burdens. After a moment or two, Ansell murmured, without looking towards MacConnachie,

'Just as long as you didn't hang about here for my benefit. I don't need any favours.'

There was silence, then the voice came back.

'I do nothing for your benefit that isn't for my benefit too.'

'Right.'

'Right.'

MacConnachie brushed past to take up the lead.

'Stay close. When it gets lighter we'll move up on to the ridge.'

'We'll show on the skyline.'

'Not till dawn.'

'Give me the gun.

'What?'

Ansell took it, fiddled with it, and handed it back.

'It's still on single-shot.'

'Thank you.'

MacConnachie started to move, then turned back.

'Tomorrow will be better.'

It was already tomorrow.

As they worked their way cautiously along to the right, mounting steadily closer to the peak, their spirits rose in the cool night air, and their pace quickened. Within an hour they were walking upright, taking no more than normal precautions.

Ansell knew that the first physical and psychological barriers had been surmounted for, although his body ached still, he found that with each moment he marched more strongly and easily.

MacConnachie, it was clear, possessed the gift, invaluable in the circumstances, of surrender without inhibition to his animal instincts: if it rained, he took shelter; if he was hungry, he ate; if in danger, he killed. And he could sleep, if tired, even in the cannon's mouth, when there was nothing to be gained by moving.

To think too much, Ansell decided, is to undo yourself. You scheme, you worry, you try to take everything into account, and you become inhibited. You fail to act. Action is the key to survival. Emulate MacConnachie.

By five, in MacConnachie's estimation, they had travelled fifteen miles, and contact was decisively broken. That was the key to survival. If they could remain out of contact for three days, they had a chance.

There are times when it's better to do nothing, but I'm no thinker. The kid'll have to do my thinking for me.

'Sleep now. We've done well.'

Ansell checked the gun and they slept.

MacConnachie woke with dawn on the fourth day. He had chosen well. They lay in a small depression on the forward slope of the main ridge, just below the skyline, where they could not be approached, under cover, from any direction. Savouring a sense of harmony with his surroundings, he followed the progress of light down into the low ground, until he could see the entire area ahead.

Immediately to his front, a day's march away, was a smaller ridge that formed the false horizon. This he christened Little Ridge, and designated in his mind their day's objective. Beyond, he could see the peaks of the mountains against a colourless sky, and stirred with excitement to have them so close.

Between Little Ridge and Big Ridge, the name he gave to the crest on which they lay, there was a stretch of terrain so fragmented that it might have been smashed by a giant hammer, and so heavily grown with scrub that it could only indicate a big river system between the hills and the mountains. It was territory fraught with danger for them, since it offered innumerable hiding-places to their enemies, and no clear view forward to themselves.

He had just decided that they should eat and commit themselves at once when he saw the figures below: the first of the Goons who lay in wait across their front.

There was no mistaking them. Small and busy, they were shaking down for the new day; just visible on the far side of a medium height, near the top, about two hours' march away and directly below. It appeared that they must have slept in low ground, and this bothered him by virtue of its obvious military ineptness. He searched at once for sentries or for another party, reaching out a hand to wake Ansell as he did so. Ansell said,

'That's cosy.'

'Look for an advance party. There must be one. That lot are too casual.'

'Right.'

They searched the terrain in silence, then Ansell suddenly gripped his arm.

'Mac, there!'

The figures were coming up in single file, about half a mile to their right, close now to the top of the ridge. They counted until all had appeared.

'Eleven.'

'With a radio.'

'Eleven's too many.'

'See which way they search.'

They waited as the climbing figures laboured upwards. Every now and then MacConnachie glanced down at the main party below, but there was no sign of a move by them. It was impossible to guess how many other Goons were hidden behind the height, but certainly there were some, perhaps a fair number, to judge by the way the visible members of the force kept talking and gesturing down to them.

Then the buzz of the helicopter came to them from somewhere away to their left, and MacConnachie said,

'See what he's doing.'

'I'll have to move.'

'Watch your rear.'

As Ansell wriggled away, MacConnachie watched the advance party achieve the summit. The radio operator adjusted his aerial and reported back to the main force. Looking down, MacConnachie saw that his opposite number had appeared on top of the height below, evidently increasing his elevation to prevent any masking of signals. Once the report was complete, the entire advance party sat down, lit cigarettes, and chatted among themselves.

Ten minutes passed, and then the tiny figures on the height below suddenly straightened up, as at a word of command, and doubled down out of sight. MacConnachie waited to see in which direction, once the full force had emerged, the search would set out. Whichever way they moved, the advance party also would move, along the top of the ridge where he and Ansell lay.

Ansell rejoined him.

'The chopper's searching the front face of the ridge, well away to our left. The River Boys are about two thirds of the way up the scarp. There are dozens more of them now.'

'There would be.'

'I estimate two hundred. They're coming fast, in sections. I think they're going to fan out.'

'You can count on it.'

Ansell looked past him at the advance party.

'Nip along and see if they've got a couple of fags to spare, Mac. You're better at that sort of thing than I am.'

MacConnachie said, 'Look.'

A single file of men had begun to appear from behind the height below. The leading Goon brought them round hard right, and led them towards the ridge. Ansell said,

'That's jolly.'

'They won't come up here. They'll move left or right in extended order. The question is, which?'

Twenty men in all appeared in the first column, and when the leading man had satisfied himself that the last man had emerged, he held up his hand and the file halted.

'That can't be the lot.'

'Not a chance.'

A second file appeared, this time wheeling hard left and marching away from them, until a further twenty men had attached themselves to the end of the first column. The entire line then turned to face towards MacConnachie and Ansell's right.

'Thank God for that.'

The extended formation moved off, working their way conscientiously forward, poking into every patch of brush with fixed bayonets. The advance party had also risen and, as the searchers progressed below, they kept pace with them along the top of the ridge. At the end of twenty minutes, three columns of forty men each had appeared and moved off in the wake of the leading line, sweeping up. All they could see now of the advance party was an occasional isolated figure negotiating one of the bumps along the ridge.

'Just so long as they keep going in that direction.'

'They're bound to turn eventually.'

'We'll be across the valley by then. That's Little Ridge, today's objective. This is Big Ridge. Let's eat and move.'

They had half a tin of meat for breakfast, and made another unsuccessful attempt to defecate.

'I wanted to half an hour ago.'

'It'll come.'

'I wish it would hurry up,' said Ansell wretchedly. He had been troubled by bouts of dizziness brought on by constipation, which he hated. He was an orderly man, and this was part of order. He saw, too, that MacConnachie was filthy, pale faced and heavily grown with beard. He must look the same. He probably smelt as well. It was the first time since his imprisonment that he had thought of his appearance and yet, although by nature neat and scrupulously clean, he was not so disconcerted by their squalid condition as he would have expected. On the contrary, it made him feel tougher, more competent, closer to MacConnachie.

Inspecting his hands in extension of these thoughts, he turned them over and caught sight of his finger-nails. Not one remained unbroken. Some were torn off more than halfway down. Others were split vertically to the cuticle. His stomach stirred uneasily at the mixture of blood and dirt encrusted together, but he felt no pain. He said,

'Should we do something about our hands?'

MacConnachie inspected Ansell's fingers with gentle impatience, and then his own. He grinned.

'Leave 'em. If we wash 'em, they'll hurt. Anyway, the dirt will protect them.'

MacConnachie packed the half-tin of meat they hadn't eaten,

and roped up the case while Ansell checked the gun. They then had a mouthful of water apiece, and set out once more.

But for one unfortunate development, the first half of the morning was trouble free. They progressed with steady caution along defiles, up gullies, and through thickets of scrub. Twice they took cover at false alarms, once, they saw a species of creature neither could identify. But, despite a careful watch for observation posts in the high ground, they saw no sign of the enemy, nor did they find evidence of his passing. Apart from the persistent buzz of the helicopter, itself distant, they might have been forgotten

Then, about ten o'clock, the unfortunate development occurred. Ansell suddenly stopped, and crouched.

'Mac! I've got the squitters!'

MacConnachie turned back and roared with laughter.

'Oh, no!'

Ansell's face contracted as a spasm passed through him and relief came.

'It isn't funny!'

'It is, you know. I've been holding 'em in for half an hour.'

Suddenly MacConnachie too crouched.

'Oh God!'

His first spasm passed, meeting Ansell's second.

'It was that bloody fruit!'

'I know.'

MacConnachie couldn't stop laughing. Ansell looked about in alarm, and moaned,

'Oh God, this is hopeless!'

But then he too started to laugh. Their situation was so ridiculous. They squatted opposite one another, completely unprotected, the skirts of their native coats around their waists, gaining relief at one end, and then, through laughter, at the other, alternately. At least they had been without underwear since their capture, and their slacks were tied about their waists. Otherwise the damage would have been intolerable.

In time, the worst excesses of laughter and diarrhoea passed, and they were able to progress again. But they had to stop repeatedly for one or the other to crouch, and it wasn't until nearly midday that they finally regained control of their tender stomachs. During one of their latter halts, MacConnachie grinned down at the squatting Ansell and said, solemnly,

'I suppose you realize you're leaving a trail.'

Ansell said,

'I hope the Goons take it in the spirit in which it is offered.'

Midday. They were approximately halfway between Big and Little Ridges, when Ansell saw tiny figures on Little Ridge, their day's objective, near the peak. For the first time they were surrounded. The way ahead was blocked.

MacConnachie moved at once, crouching, to the nearest rising feature, where he lay looking up at the enemy. Ansell joined him.

'What do we do?'

'Keep moving. We must. The River Boys will soon hit the top of Big Ridge. We're in broken ground, that helps.'

'Which way?'

'Straight ahead. Why not?'

For the next hour they wormed their way closer and closer to Little Ridge, MacConnachie leading, Ansell maintaining distance. But it took only a fraction of that time for the breaking strain to close over them again. Time after time they thought they had been spotted and tensed to run—but they hadn't been. They sought frustratedly a clear view of their enemy. Each open area became something to crawl across: gullies had to be walked, never upright, as though strewn with eggs, so urgent was the need to prevent drifting dust; defiles were cracks in the earth up which they slunk. In seconds only, the deportment of a man became the stealth of an animal.

Then they saw what the Goons were doing.

A line of men had formed up in extended order across their front, at the foot of Little Ridge. On a word of command they turned to face towards MacConnachie and Ansell, fixed bayonets and, at the next bark, moved slowly towards them, fanning out, thrusting the steel into every patch of brush and scrub.

Behind this line there was another, some yards up the ridge still, and after that a third. These, in their turn, would form up when they reached the valley floor and, by following in the wake of the first, create a lateral sweep, three layers deep, of searching steel. MacConnachie murmured,

'Christ!'

'That is awkward.'

'Yes.'

MacConnachie was twisting his head this way and that, looking urgently to right and left and behind him. Ansell said,

'Which way?'

'We'll have to go back!'

'Surely not?'

'What then?'

It seemed to Ansell there was a new element in MacConnachie suddenly, not of fear exactly, but of desperation. He himself felt startlingly calm. He looked along the line of approaching men, left and right. They were about a hundred yards away, but he and MacConnachie were much closer to the right-hand end of the line than they were to the centre. He said,

'Let's try to get round the end.'

'Which one?'

'Right flank.'

MacConnachie looked and said,

'We'd never make it.'

'Well, where do we go, if we go backwards?'

Again MacConnachie looked, blinking the sweat out of his eyes. The Goons kept appearing and disappearing in different places, always closer to them, as they worked their way over the humpback of the terrain. At length, snappishly, MacConnachie said,

'We'd be going closer to the enemy!'

'For Christ's sake—we're surrounded! We can't do anything else!'

All the time the net drew tighter, their chances diminished, and MacConnachie hesitated. Ansell couldn't understand it. He was about to break forth in rage, when MacConnachie said, quietly,

'What do we do if we don't make it?'

There was such sadness in his tone that Ansell looked at him closely.

'We lie still and hope for the best.'

MacConnachie nodded.

'That's what I thought,' he said.

And now Ansell understood, and felt pity for the older man, who lay staring glumly at the safety to their right. He had immeasurable courage to stand and fight, to pit his strength against mountains and rivers and sun. But to lie and wait, to leave his death to chance, deliberately to relinquish the initiative, and with it his dignity as a fighter, was beyond him. Ansell didn't know what to do.

'Mac, we've got to move!'

'I know.'

MacConnachie was unable to look at him.

Ansell said, 'Come on,' and immediately scrambled away to his right, not looking back to see if MacConnachie followed. For ten minutes he didn't look back; it became a point of honour. He concentrated solely on the job in hand, an immensely difficult manoeuvre complicated by the fact that he never knew at what point a Goon face might suddenly appear above him. At a half-crouch he hobbled along, wallowing in tacky sweat, stopping again and again to peer gropingly, to wait, to listen, sometimes seeing many men, sometimes none. Now he was afraid; the unnatural calm had left him, and he felt intensely alone. The heat bore down and the earth pressed up to meet him.

It became rapidly apparent that he would never make the end of the line before it was upon him. He looked, at last, for MacConnachie, but MacConnachie was nowhere to be seen. He told himself that this was due to the nature of the ground, but his determination wilted, and he began to seek a place to hide.

Every movement was stiff with caution now. Figures lurched into view not thirty yards away, and snatches of conversation came to him. He wriggled to a gully and, sliding into it, burrowed deep into the thick scrub. With one cheek pressed against the cool soil, he waited, straining his ears for the slightest sound. But it was no good. Whatever training may decree about the white flash of a face in shadow, he was unable to accept the prospect of lying there, face down, to be bayoneted in the back. He turned with great caution to face whatever came, looking up into the impenetrable brush.

The sound of voices was loud now, and the swishing of boots through scrub seemed everywhere. He clung to the canteen, suddenly pulling it, on impulse, over his stomach to protect it, wishing MacConnachie were with him, or that he knew MacConnachie was safe. As a man does, even when he can see nothing, he moved his eyes to follow the sounds that approached him.

For an immensely long time the voices were near without actually reaching him, then suddenly boots crunched by very close to his head, and he heard the swish and snick of searching metal against the branches, and the small chop of steel driving into earth. He had intended to remain alert to the last, to fight when all hope was gone, but in fact he shut his eyes and murmured, 'God, God.'

There was a startlingly loud remark in his right ear, and the first line was gone.

Silence fell, of such a pitch that he gasped. He thought, until that last moment, that he had lain calm, but now his bones creaked as they unlocked themselves from a posture so rigid it sent pains flaring down his limbs. What in the name of God had happened to MacConnachie? At the thought, his body locked again in fear, waiting for the sudden shout and the bursts of rapid fire. Then he heard the second line approaching.

No search, however deep, can be completely thorough. It is the nature of men that, seeing the man in front, they tend to probe in different places. Ansell lay in no danger from the second line, but he suffered as he had never suffered with the first.

By the time the second line had passed, Ansell knew he should never have hidden in a gully; it was the first place a searcher would look. But observation should have told him that this fact had twice been defied in the event. And common sense should have told him that no soldier, laden with equipment in the hot sun, would willingly struggle along a gully when he could walk beside it, using the length of his rifle to poke its depths with a bayonet. Ansell made up his mind to move.

Very cautiously, he eased round on to his knees, holding the canteen in front of him, searching the canopy of scrub for a place through which he might take a careful look about. He got no farther. A bayonet came down through the foliage, jarred against the canteen, knocked it from his hands, and the third line was gone. He hadn't even heard them coming but, strangely, as though in some way the close call had released their tension too, they chattered now, animatedly among themselves, as they went away.

For some moments he remained in a state of stilled shock, unmoving. Then his whole body started to tremble as he gasped with astonishment and relief, chilled by a sudden cold, then flushed by an uncomfortable and sticky warmth. He folded forward. The canteen lay a few inches from his face, a raw, livid gash in its leather work. The Goon must have thought it a rock. He laughed uneasily.

Then he began to concern himself with MacConnachie, who, to judge by the absence of shooting, must still be safe. They had to regain contact at once. After three minutes, he wriggled to the edge of the gully and looked back.

The searchers were bobbing in and out of view as they had before, but now they were moving away from him, and they looked less dangerous. There was no sign of the River Boys yet on Big Ridge, but when they came the valley search party would turn back and try their luck a second time. A small command group still remained on Little Ridge.

He had last been with MacConnachie to his left. If Mac were still on that side, then Mac would find him. He would know that Ansell couldn't move without increasing the danger of their passing one another. He waited fifteen minutes, and then another fifteen.

To the right, then. That was their last line of march. He had to increase his field of view, to get higher without being seen by the many eyes that surrounded him.

He left the gully at a flat crawl, animal-close to the earth, slithering over cracks and fissures, the torments of dust and heat forgotten, seeking a place from which to scent the hunt, the canteen dragging behind him. At last, to his left, he saw a feature that might be suitable, and inched his way to the top.

The extended lines of men had almost reached Big Ridge, and now the River Boys had appeared on the summit. In a few minutes the net would be recast, and if he and MacConnachie were still outside it, they were only just beyond its outer rim. He could see to his right a wide gully, some forty yards distant, that ran away towards Little Ridge. He decided to make for it. It was a feature so prominent that MacConnachie could hardly miss it, and would be bound to head for it in the end.

He eased down, orientated himself, and set off again to his right. The next moment he came face to face with MacConnachie, who grinned and said,

'Thought you'd get up high to see me. Wouldn't have spotted you otherwise.'

Ansell laid his face in the dust.

'God, am I glad to see you.'

'Mutual.'

He felt MacConnachie's hand rest on his shoulder.

'Are you all right?'

Ansell looked up, nodding.

'Yes.'

MacConnachie examined him a moment, then frowned.

'Come on, I've found a place.'

'I saw it.'

As he wriggled after MacConnachie, Ansell said,

'What happened to you?'

MacConnachie hesitated.

'Tell you later.'

Ansell thought that, once in the gully, MacConnachie should not have left it.

It took them twenty minutes to travel the forty yards to the gully. All the time, the numbers on Big Ridge increased as more and more of the River Boys reached the top. Once inside, Ansell said,

'Can we rest a bit? I'm clapped.'

'Sure. Have a drink.'

'You too?'

'All right.'

Solicitously, MacConnachie unstoppered and held the canteen for Ansell, who allowed the water to linger in his mouth before swallowing. He noticed that MacConnachie fingered the gash in its side, not drinking himself. Safe again, Ansell grinned.

'Close call.'

MacConnachie muttered,

'I didn't know it was that close.'

'Don't think I realized myself at the time.'

MacConnachie sat silent, drinking. Ansell looked along the gully. It was deep, scrub-thick, and gave the impression, at this distance, of reaching all the way to Little Ridge. Suddenly, un-asked, MacConnachie began to explain himself, scowling and pausing often:

'I nearly had kittens when I saw them close over you.' Silence. 'I took a hell of a chance. I ran like the clappers. Stupid. We could have been blown. But I couldn't fancy them'—he banged the stopper home with the palm of his hand—'crawling all over me. Like *ants*!' Silence. 'Hate those little men. *Hate* them!' He wasn't able to look at Ansell. 'Anyway, I found this place.' He looked instead at the place where Ansell had lain under the bayonets. He said, 'I had kittens.'

Ansell was at a loss for words.

'I had them myself.'

'I believe you.' A long silence. 'I was ... I guess maybe ... Perhaps I ... '

Ansell couldn't bear it; he had to look away.

'You did the right thing. You covered the flank. We had enfiladed fire, if we needed it.'

'That's right. I mean, I did, didn't I?' MacConnachie nodded vigorously, as though the appearance of conviction could engender the conviction itself. 'That's true.'

For something to say, Ansell said,

'They're coming towards us again.'

'We must move.'

MacConnachie was at once busy with practicalities.

'We'll go up this gully. Watch for drifting dust.'

Then he noticed that he was still holding the canteen and, with a foolish grin, re-stoppered it and handed it to Ansell.

'Let's go.'

The boy was right. Yes, he'd done the right thing. Enfiladed fire. Yes.

Ansell was visited by a comic vision, such as he had had before. It was of MacConnachie, suitcase in one hand, gun in the other, haring across the landscape, 'going like the clappers', with the skirts of his native coat flapping about his ankles; had there been a hand clasping a bonnet to the back of the head, it might have been a grandmother making a getaway.

But he was glad it was MacConnachie, and not he, who had to carry the suitcase and the gun.

As they picked their way up the gully, the day died. Shortly before nightfall they reached its end, to discover that it did not in fact extend all the way to Little Ridge, but petered out in a rash of scrub and rocky outcrop.

'Sit tight?'

'Till night, yes.'

MacConnachie considered for a moment.

'We'll eat. Soon as it's dark, we'll cross Little Ridge, and get the hell out of this valley.'

It was as though MacConnachie blamed the valley for his own defection. Ansell had had time to appreciate, and thoroughly to examine, the fact that while he had lain under the bayonets, MacConnachie had watched from a place of safety; and further, that he had achieved that safety only at the risk of jeopardizing their entire escape. Yet Ansell was unable to generate any emotion about this, either anger or a sense of betrayal. In war, what you got away with was good; what you didn't was bad.

He remembered that in every battle he had ever fought in,

some men had hidden, or run away. In the next, they hadn't, but others had. At different moments, in differing circumstances, what one man found acceptable another found intolerable. The normal conventions of praise and blame did not apply. He thought it an admirable system. Both he and MacConnachie were tired, and had enough to carry as it was.

Having eaten the meat left over from breakfast, they drank and rested, waiting for night.

At MacConnachie's word, they set out again to traverse Little Ridge. Compared to previous climbs, it was a simple ascent, and in less than two hours they were on the peak, lying flat and peering forward into the night. Of the enemy they saw and heard nothing, though they knew him to be close. Of the country ahead they saw little more, save patches of shadow accentuated by the pale glow in the sky. MacConnachie put his face close to Ansell's.

'We'll go as far and as fast as we can, then rest.'

Ansell nodded exaggeratedly, to be sure MacConnachie caught the movement.

Very quickly it became apparent that they were leaving the range of hills. Counting tomorrow, they would have made the march in five days, two less than estimated; MacConnachie was pleased. The ground continued gently and steadily downhill, and they made fast time.

Then came the moment when MacConnachie's feet told him that the nature of the earth had changed; and shortly afterwards his nostrils confirmed it. They were not far from water. They must stop. Before he led them out of the hills, he needed to see the ground ahead.

At the next gentle rise, he cast about for a place to sleep; once he had found it, they bedded down.

He was concerned. The next day, he knew, he could feel,

would face them with their second area of maximum danger, and he had a great need to feel that both his hands were free; but the suitcase had to be carried. So he looked down at the boy who slept peacefully in the security of his trust, and fretted.

The fifth dawn found MacConnachie already awake, waiting impatiently for the mist to clear. His whole body prickled with a sense of dissonance relative to the territory around him. Something was wrong. He shook Ansell.

'What's up?'

'We've got to move.'

Ansell peered blearily at the mist.

'Have we been seen?'

'No. Something's wrong, I can feel it.'

Ansell was awake at once. Just the word 'feel' communicated the urgency to him: MacConnachie's instinct had become, for him, hope itself. Rapidly, he repacked their jackets and blanket.

'Eat now?'

'Later.'

He roped up the case and laid it at MacConnachie's other side. Then he tested the weight of the canteen on first one shoulder, then the other. The left was still by far the more painful so, draping the strap over his right, he rested his hand lightly on the knife, quietly waiting MacConnachie's order.

The mist was maddeningly slow to lift, for they were much lower down than hitherto, and MacConnachie shifted restively all the time. Then, quite suddenly the drifting wraiths were gone, and he could see to his rear.

They had walked on to the stage of a natural amphitheatre, a wide, shallow basin in the face of the slope. To left, right, and behind they were overlooked by a horseshoe of ground higher than that on which they lay—though not so high that MacConnachie could have seen it, by night, against the pale glow. The Goons had only to man the heights, close the neck of the horseshoe, and they would be trapped. Speed was essential.

Ansell muttered, 'Christ,' and, turning, MacConnachie saw that he was looking into the ground that lay ahead. A glance gave him a quick impression of cultivated fields, a river system and the mountains beyond, but looking farther to his right he saw that on that side the arm of the horseshoe crumpled away into a confused area of high scrub and trees, where the ground fell away steeply into the valley. He said, 'Run! Don't stop!'

They ran flat out, completely exposed to view, until they fell among the tall scrub and tangled branches of the thicket. Just before they reached it, without any warning, the helicopter suddenly roared down out of the thin morning sky, scudding low over the crest of Little Ridge and swishing past above them.

Ansell could not believe it. It was too fortuitous to be chance, and yet he could not accept the possibility that they had been spotted in the valley the day before. That would mean that the Goons had known all the time where they were, and were using their escape to test their own techniques of search and destroy. If that were true, it was the end of him. Unlike MacConnachie, he could not endure without prospect of reward. If he were simply the object of sport, he did not want to go on. Demoralized and chill, he lay dazed with fear, inwardly weeping.

Then he heard the voice of MacConnachie, weary and defiant, murmuring a litany of such outraged and convolute obscenity that small eructations of helpless laughter bubbled up in him like wind. What's the use? he thought.

Together they rose to peer through the umbrella of branches.

'What's the little bastard up to?'

'Setting a pattern over the forward slopes.'

'We might as well eat.'

'Did he see us?'

'I don't know.'

'How did he know where to search?'

'Because he's good.' Again, Ansell heard the note of amused comradeship in MacConnachie's voice. 'He knew we'd left the valley. He knows we're good too.'

'What do we do?'

'Assume he didn't see us.'

MacConnachie turned away, and started to untie the suitcase. Ansell said,

'Can we afford to?'

'Kid, we haven't any choice. We've got to eat; the worst is just ahead of us. And there's nothing we can do, either way.'

MacConnachie pulled a tin out of the case, and took the kitchen knife to it. Far from satisfied, Ansell sat on the scab grass opposite him. The scrub was much taller than any they had so far encountered, the branches interleaving in a roof above their heads. A withered, spiky tree grew close at hand and, farther down the slope, the worn and twisted trunks of other trees were visible between the strands of meshing brush. The buzz of the helicopter apart, it was a peaceful glade. They had half a tin of meat for breakfast, and a mouthful of water each. Then, in preparation for what was to come, they examined their physical capacity.

MacConnachie's wrist, where the rope had burned it, was suppurating a little, or had been, for the cloth with which Ansell had bound it was stuck fast. Ansell said,

'Hang on a sec, I'll give it one quick heave.'

MacConnachie recoiled in alarm.

'Are you out of your mind?!'

'You want to see what it looks like.'

'Sod what it looks like! I can't feel it, it must be all right.'

Ansell laughed.

'I'll bet you're scared of jabs as well.'

'Who isn't? Anyway, why open it? We've nothing to put on it.'

'We can clean it.'

'I'll keep it the way it is!'

Silence. Then Ansell said,

'Mac, you can't really not feel it, can you?'

MacConnachie glowered at him like an evil-tempered child, then waggled his hand from the wrist. 'It's all right.' Finally a look of resignation appeared on his face. 'Oh, all right, then!' He seized the cloth and ripped it off with one jerk.

The sides of the channel burnt in the flesh were thickly encrusted with congealed pus and blood. At the centre, a colourless fluid rose up before their eyes to glisten in the diffused light of the clearing. Flies came at once to settle and feed, but Ansell flushed them away. MacConnachie tossed the cloth aside, and instantly it was black with gorging insects.

Ansell put his nose to the wound and smelt it.

'Well?'

'It's clean.' Ansell reached for the canteen, saying, 'Don't argue, I just want to use a little to wash it.'

MacConnachie nodded.

'All right.'

Ansell took another section of torn-off sleeve and, with great care, washed the waste from MacConnachie's wound, gradually breaking off little pieces of the harder substance, until the area was seen to be fresh, uncorrupt, and far better than they had feared. Finally, he dampened the cloth again, slit one end down the centre with the kitchen knife, and bound it round Mac-Connachie's wrist, tying off the ends.

'That should be okay,' he said; 'I don't think there's any danger of … '

But he decided not to mention gangrene.

MacConnachie checked that the canteen was securely stoppered, and then examined Ansell. The one thing that gave him real concern was Ansell's left shoulder.

Both of them had suffered superficial damage to their arms, legs and faces; and of course there were debilitating factors, such as lack of food and sleep, about which they could do nothing. But the shoulder was another matter.

On the first day, the strap must have bitten deeply. The skin was chafed and rubbed away from neck to shoulder, and even now had begun only improperly to re-form. The worst weals were in the centre, puffy and bruised across the ridge of bone; from there, they radiated outwards with diminishing severity, as the boy must have shifted the canteen from place to place in a vain search for relief.

So far as he could see the area was not actually weeping, but carrying the canteen must have become an agony that could only grow worse. A quick glance at the other shoulder told him that soon there would be nothing to choose between the two. The boy had not complained. Well, the canteen had to be carried. He said,

'Not too bad.'

'The right's better.'

'Try draping it round your neck.'

'I've been meaning to, but we seem to crawl all the time.'

'It'll be better when we get in the mountains.'

'Yes.'

But MacConnachie could not push the memory of that ravaged shoulder from his mind. Knowing he would have to approach the suggestion obliquely, unsubtle though he was, he nodded briskly and turned away, saying,

'We'll see if we can find something to pad it with.' And then, very casual, 'I'll give you a spell, when I can, to give it a chance to heal.'

'Thank you.'

'Good. That's fixed.'

'And I'll take the suitcase.'

Oh well.

The water had made Ansell's finger-tips tingle, reminding him of their condition, but, having so recently seen the produce of MacConnachie's wound, he decided against interfering with his own. Their boots had stood the march well, remaining weatherproof and securely attached all round. And this time, when they scratched out their shallow holes and squatted, they were both successful.

'Must be the early morning trot.'

'We'll ask him to call us again tomorrow.'

Finally, MacConnachie said,

'We must move to a place where we can see the whole valley ahead.'

It took nearly half an hour to find a suitable position. Crawling down through the scrub, they came suddenly upon a dazzling complex of brush, creeper and vine, at the heart of which, and running to its forward edge, there lay a scab-grown depression, offering concealment and a perfect vista of the valley floor. Settling on his stomach, MacConnachie read the ground over which they must travel; to know it by heart was essential.

From left to right, a river system of four elements ran across their front. The valley floor itself was cultivated and well in- habited, being dotted with huts. Beyond, the mountains rose sheer into the sky.

He broke this panorama down into its component parts.

From their present position to the level valley floor was a distance of about a mile. Gentle downhill slope. Cover, fair to middling, with enough isolated scrub to offer a reasonable passage to the valley. Here the fields began, with hedging dykes beyond, and deep cover abundant.

The valley floor was a mile and a half across. The main river ran along its entire length, with two tributaries on the far side, and one on this, his own side. This nearer stream curled back on itself, running towards the hills and petering out. But the farther two, maintaining a bolder passage, ran more or less parallel to the main river until, with it, they disappeared from view behind the swell of the hillside to his right.

At the other, left-hand end of the valley, the four streams came together to form a delta. But here there was a permanent Goon station, and the thickest concentration of those huts that proliferated all about the water system.

They would have, therefore, three hazards of water to cross, one wide and two narrow. Selecting a route that took best advantage of the distribution of huts, jetties and river traffic, MacConnachie memorized it, and turned his attention to that part of the valley that lay outside the rivers on either side.

A simple pattern emerged at once. Wherever the valley floor failed to support either water or a home, it was cultivated, the fields reaching out towards the hills and mountains, into which they were cut and shelved until the soil became intransigent.

He was puzzled by the exact nature of some of the crops. Those fields, for instance, that lay in their direct line of march to the river appeared to be full of a wheat-like growth that stood, unless he was mistaken, over eight feet tall. He turned to Ansell.

'What the hell's that stuff?'

'Which?'

'In the fields, dead ahead. Looks like corn.'

'Bloody big corn. Higher than the chap beside it.

'Um…'

To this could be added the animation of life—pigs, water-buffalo, chickens, ducks, people, all with the soaring mountains beyond—and the picture was complete.

Or nearly.

For it was MacConnachie's method, when time allowed, to assimilate first the territory itself, with its natural accretions of indigenous habitation, and then to place within this framework the more recently acquired dispositions of his enemies. This was based on his unquestioned and instinctive knowledge that Nature is on a man's side, if he knows how to woo her. It is only when a man is caught without knowledge of his surroundings, or with indifference to them, or with an active enmity to them, that he is defeated: Nature is waiting and willing to be loved. Properly cared for, she makes the ideal woman: permissive, protective, productive, and helpful. A man is a fool not to take hands with her.

He placed his enemy in his mind. From the Goon station on the delta, there flowed a steady trickle of three-man patrols, which set out along the valley floor to throw a thin, perpetually shifting barrier across their front.

There was also a larger fighting patrol, forty strong, moving freely in the area they were about to cross, between the hillside and the tall fields. But they were well to the left and, given luck, he and Ansell should bypass them altogether.

Of course, the chopper was still in the sky behind them, and the net of infantry was drawing closer, but there was nothing he could do about that. The essence of a successful valley crossing was to be seen by no one, uniformed or otherwise. Once committed to a fire fight, they would not survive; the potential build-up of Goon manpower was too great.

Given a choice, he would have crossed by night. But there was no choice.

'Kid, when we hit that valley, nothing stops us. *Nothing!* We shoot, we kill, but we *must get across!* We stop when we're dead, not before. Okay?'

'Right.'

'We'll worry about replenishing stores from the other side. Once we're on the valley floor, we walk upright. Till then, we take our chances. One more thing. Local militia. If you see a bloke who looks like a farmer out for a day's sport—we're the sport.'

'No uniform?'

'Goon clobber, just like ours. And maybe an old elephant gun. Watch those things, they serve you up diced for lunch.'

'Well, one of us would have a decent meal.'

'Let's get what we can hidden under our coats.'

MacConnachie loosened the sling of the gun and draped it round his neck so that the weapon hung down through the full opening of the coat, making a bulge under the material. He then seized the whole arrangement and gave it a thorough shaking— like a monk with a cold crucifix against his skin—until it had fallen into natural folds and a comfortable disposition. Ansell did the same with the canteen. There was nothing they could do about the suitcase. Picking it up, MacConnachie grinned.

'If anyone asks, I'll say we're commercial travellers.'

'In ladies' underwear?'

'Let's go.'

For the next hour they fell into a routine which, by virtue of its sheer professionalism, carried them safely through a most delicate manoeuvre. MacConnachie would select their next hide and indicate it to Ansell. Then, while MacConnachie examined every inch of visible terrain for movement, Ansell would calculate the helicopter's flight. As soon as MacConnachie said the ground was clear, they both waited for Ansell's word of command, which Ansell based on the estimated visibility from the helicopter at a given moment. When he shouted 'Now!' they fled from each cover to the next without stopping.

To this they had added a safety factor. They always crouched back to back, MacConnachie between Ansell and the next target feature. Thus, if anything obtruded into MacConnachie's field of vision between his all clear and Ansell's 'Now!' he was able to hold Ansell back to the very last moment.

This mechanism never had to be engaged. The combination of Ansell's perception and MacConnachie's instinct proved sufficient.

As they worked their way down the hillside, two factors became increasingly significant, both brought about by a steady thickening in the vegetation through which they moved: on the one hand, they became harder to spot; on the other, their own field of vision diminished all the time.

At length the slope levelled off, and they knew they were approaching the first fields. So far they had seen few people, none of them Goon soldiers. But each person represented a pair of eyes, and while few civilians would have the courage to apprehend them, none would lack the courage to report them.

They crouched side by side, and peered through the scrub. Immediately ahead was the edge of the first field, running across their front and presenting a solid wall of close-packed stalks to their gaze. The intervening space was alive with flying insects, hovering in the air, darting about, coming to drink at their streaked faces, swarming maddeningly. The heat of the day was building up, the familiar burden of the sun lay heavy upon them, and within the muffling folds of their garments they sweated without pause.

So far as they could see, the field stretched for about a hundred and fifty yards to their left. To the right, it ended abruptly at a narrow track some thirty feet distant, on the far side of which were the corner and walls of another exactly similar field, which twisted and wound away to disappear from view behind the scrub.

It was reasonable to assume that other tracks led down into the valley somewhere to their left, but at this distance they received the impression of a continuing wall of stalks, as though one field ran into the next without demarcation. MacConnachie muttered,

'I don't fancy that lot. It'll show from above. Let's try the track.'

They wriggled through the clutching undergrowth until they came to the corner of the field. MacConnachie raised his hand and Ansell stopped. With extreme caution, MacConnachie edged forward, face against the earth, until he could see round the intervening stalks.

One of the three-man patrols was wandering idly up the track towards them, guns at the trail, its members chatting in a desultory way with a group of armed farmers. They were two minutes distant.

As cautiously as he had extended his head—to make a sudden movement is to draw the searching eye—MacConnachie withdrew it.

It wasn't until he turned that Ansell knew anything was amiss. MacConnachie whispered,

'We've had it. They're coming up the track.' He nodded towards the dangerous, towering stalks. 'We'll have to take to the long grass.'

Ansell knew at once that this was the moment of greatest danger. Inside that jungle they would be blind. He glanced fearfully to his left.

'Haven't we time to get down there?'

'No. Now do exactly as I do.'

MacConnachie rose, looked to his rear, then extended his arms straight ahead, passing them between two of the boundary stalks and as deeply into the growth as he could. Then he extended them outwards, bending the stalks apart from the base, and opening a passage into which it was possible for him to step. He looked back over his shoulder.

'Toss in the case.'

Ansell took the suitcase, squeezed in front of MacConnachie's arched body, and threw it gently down among the bowed stalks. MacConnachie said,

'Once I'm in, do the same beside me.'

Lifting his feet high, MacConnachie stepped in after the suitcase and, by drawing his arms behind him and letting them fall, allowed the stalks to come together at his back. He had vanished completely. The stalks might never have been disturbed. The effect was of a stunning theatrical illusion.

Astonished, Ansell did the same, parting the stalks and stepping among them. The two men had disappeared.

Inside the field, they were in a different world. Ansell had had no idea the stalks grew so close together. It was just possible to find room for his feet between them, but his body was caged like a vessel in wickerwork, and every time he moved, as he did now to look about for MacConnachie, the crisp susurration of friction was set up between his shoulders and the dried-out stalks.

So close to his face, these had the appearance of rigid, soured bananas, immensely long and straight, with many brownish scars deeply ingrained in their cracked yellow surfaces, up and down which there hurried hundreds of minute creatures in disordered files. The sense of confinement, of oppression, was intense. He looked to the sky in an attempt to draw clear breath, but only a small patch of that colourless expanse was visible, directly above, between the reaching fingers of the stalks.

He needed desperately to have some contact with MacConnachie, even though he knew him to be close. He whispered: 'Mac? Mac?'

There was no reply. His whole body began to prickle. He stared fascinated at the little creatures so close to his face, so busy, and the conviction grew suddenly in him that they were swarming up his legs, crawling over his stomach, working their way into his armpits and his crutch. When a tickle crept down his cheek, he nearly screamed; but it was a bubble of oily sweat, nothing more.

Voices came to him, faintly, and he realized for the first time how quiet their new world was; he hadn't been aware of noise before, but now he was conscious of a filtering blanket of hush. And of a terrible smell that worked against his throat, creating an acrid, acidulous irritation that he was unable to swallow down. It seemed to weep from the stalks in a pungent, invisible vapour, pervasive and nauseating. He called again, louder, 'Mac?'

'*Shut up!*'

It was a harsh whisper, loaded with urgency. Ansell knew at once that something was wrong, and the next moment realized that, however distant the Goon voices might sound, they were in reality close, and MacConnachie was listening to what they said. Suddenly MacConnachie's face burst through the barrier of stalks.

'We've got to go farther in. We were seen. Swim!'

Ansell understood what he meant. By operating their arms as before, in the manner of the breast stroke, they could cleave a way through the forest of stalks, and close their tracks behind them.

At once he moved across, spreading the stalks and stepping through to join MacConnachie, who had turned his back and was trying, with as little noise and disturbance as possible, to open a way ahead. Ansell closed right up behind him so that, as MacConnachie stepped through, he could take over the strain of the bending stalks, follow MacConnachie, and then close the gap to their rear.

Three times they executed this manoeuvre, then the gun fired. MacConnachie fell at once. For an instant Ansell thought he had been hit, then saw that he was taking cover and dropped beside him.

The gun discharged an entire magazine in one long burst. At once it was joined by other guns, and the air became livid with the sounds of singing bullets, shattering stalks, and the dull thwacks of misdirected rounds. The flying metal sped about over their heads, spinning from stalk to stalk, pattering down, littering them and the area for many yards about with spent ammunition. An occasional piece of hot metal scorched them, but otherwise they remained unhurt. MacConnachie took advantage of the racket to shout,

'Soon as they stop, we go again. Some bloody farmer saw us up the hill!'

As abruptly as it had started, the shooting stopped. Voices came to them raised in consternation, and then they heard an entirely new sort of crackling: the force of the bullets had set that corner of the field ablaze.

It was apparent at once that the stuff would burn like petrol; this late in the hot season, it was fiercely combustible. The roar of spreading fire built up with astonishing speed, and the first low smoke seeped through to them. MacConnachie shouted,

'We'll have to go like the clappers! Move!'

He was up and away, bullocking through the recalcitrant stalks, smashing down anything that stood in his path. To leave his hands free, he had taken the handle of the case between his teeth. Ansell thought he had never seen him more determined or more savagely angry. He followed in his furiously created wake.

MacConnachie knew that everything now depended on speed. If they failed to beat either the fire or the Goons to the far perimeter, they were done. The Goons would throw a cordon round the field as quickly as they could, and soon the chopper would come to pin-point them.

But it takes time to set a trap, and in that time, however long or short, lay their survival.

They blundered, pitching and stumbling through the stalks, like animals in terror. They seemed to have set a thousand insects free, and, every time they gulped in air, they swallowed a fur of pulped bodies. The black specks built up like paste round their eyes, mouths and nostrils, and the sharp, tangy taste tormented Ansell, filling him with revulsion.

Again and again their boots, plunging forward, struck not earth but the tilted edge of a stalk, skidding off, throwing them sideways or back into the surrounding sticks. Progress was intolerably difficult, the press of heat within the jungle fiercely oppressive. And all the time the dancing sky teased them with glimpses of a freedom beyond their reach.

Ansell had no idea where they were; he followed MacConnachie blindly.

By now the destructiveness of their passage had turned against them, for the stalks, as they broke, presented dozens of jagged edges that lacerated their arms and shoulders, leaving slivers of shredded cane embedded in the flesh. They bled freely.

After no more than a minute or two, they were so torn and winded they had to stop. MacConnachie sagged against the stalks, unlocking his jaw to let the case fall, and sucked in great gasps of insect-packed air, his entire face, especially round the nostrils, clogged with the press of tiny bodies. Ansell did the same, his brain setting up a sort of high-pitched scream of interference, to prevent the full realization of what he swallowed from getting through.

As soon as the edge of their immediate exhaustion diminished a little, the sounds of the fire came through to them again. They were shocked to hear how close it sounded, as though they hadn't moved at all, or the fire was travelling faster than they were. Chests still heaving, they looked up and saw the thin stain of smoke sweep past overhead, rushing towards the same destination as themselves. Faster or no, the fire was travelling in the same direction, and must be spreading sideways as well.

MacConnachie snatched up the suitcase, thrust the handle between his teeth, and they crashed forward once more.

A few minutes later, the helicopter found them. The veering disturbance of their progress must have been unmistakable from above.

The first they knew of its arrival was a swirling wind that clamped the nearest stalks about their bodies, and whipped the flecked air into a churning vortex. They glared up and just caught sight of the dull-painted machine as it waddled forward, blades flashing, to disappear from view beyond the straining tips of the stalks.

As the wind passed, the stalks jostled and fretted against one another in the stress of returning equilibrium. MacConnachie looked back a moment, but there was nothing to be said.

Perhaps MacConnachie was growing tired, but it became apparent to Ansell that he was trying to give their floundering progress the appearance of a more measured passage. He had started to time his thrusts, executing them boldly and cleanly, exuding an aura of powerful, professional competence. Imitating him, Ansell found that fear diminished and, against all reason, confidence returned.

The helicopter came back to settle over their heads, blanketing all other sound with the roar of its engine, following sluggishly in their wake. At once the stalks were lashed into activity again, threshing furiously about as they were torn this way and that by the fluctuating down-draught. Progress became teeteringly slow and painful, the maelstrom threatening constantly to suck them off balance, to pitch them forward, or to hold them back and—by suddenly releasing its grip—cause them to be thrown down against the earth. And all the time the stalks lashed them, cracking down across their shoulders, breaking fiercely against their knuckles, beating them in the face, bruising their eyes, and, when they lowered their heads for protection, buffeting their crowns repeatedly. But they staggered on, MacConnachie obviously exerting every ounce of muscle and self-control to maintain his persistent, measured action.

And then Ansell understood suddenly what he was doing. Since the pilot could see them, MacConnachie was waging a psychological war, blatantly advertising the fact that he did not accept the dominance of the pilot's position, insisting with his body that the initiative lay with them. It was an act of such arrogant insolence that Ansell felt uplifted with joy. The man was indestructible.

All at once the helicopter began to step up its harassing tactics, dropping lower, pulling out and sweeping back, trying to exert pressure on them; and MacConnachie was puzzled as to why. The pilot was too good to start that nonsense without reason—certainly he hadn't been goaded into it; and yet, although he disguised his intention well, managing to give the impression that each jink and turn was caused by some natural phenomenon such as gusting wind, it was clear to MacConnachie that the pilot was perturbed. Why? They couldn't be near the edge of the field yet; it simply didn't *feel* like it.

And then, just like that, without warning, they fell out of the constricting stalks on to cropped field, with shoots no more than three inches high. It was so unexpected that they literally fell, shocked and blinking, blinded by the sudden piercing brightness of the sunlight.

As their eyes adjusted to the glare, they heard the chopper roar into a turn and bear down on them again. Ansell tried to make out the nature of the ground on which they crouched, while MacConnachie, he noticed, slipped the gun from under his tunic.

The cropping extended for about five feet, then there was a shallow irrigation canal of some kind, eight to ten feet across, with a further five feet of cropping on its far side, and beyond that the stalks rising up again across their front. They seemed to have come out into the side of a corridor that ran right across the field, down which they could look to left and right for a considerable distance before it turned on to a new path and cut off their view.

Without having seen one before, Ansell knew what it was.

'It's a fire-break!'

MacConnachie looked at him and roared with laughter.

Of course. That was why. The pilot wanted to keep them pegged in that part of the field that was ablaze. But there was more to it than that. There must be a gap. One end of the fire-break was still open, the cordon was incomplete. But which?

With the roaring and moaning of the flames growing steadily in volume at his back, and the sky dark with smoke that fled from them towards the river, MacConnachie struggled with the unaccustomed process of reasoning. The patrol that had started the fire would progress up the right flank; they must have reached the fire-break by now, and they couldn't afford to ignore it; therefore some of them at least had turned down it. Therefore it must be the left flank that was open.

The helicopter had come right down low now, the pilot stolidly waiting their move; MacConnachie could see the observer quite clearly as he talked rapidly into his mouthpiece, and the pilot leaning forward, peering at him, consumed perhaps by a similar curiosity, wanting to know the face of the man whose tenacity matched his own. MacConnachie grinned, raised two fingers in obscene salute, and shouted to Ansell, 'Come on!'

They splashed through the shallow sludge of water and mud, slopping their way over to the next wall of stalks, and, turning along it, began running down the break to their left. MacConnachie held his gun at the ready.

The helicopter reacted at once, pulling sharply back along their line of flight, coming in fast and low from behind. The next moment they were caught again in its buffeting down-draught and then, as the chopper rose away from them, a tiny cluster of tinsel-bright objects fell from it. MacConnachie seized Ansell's arm to be sure he saw them and, as they both came to a skidding halt, dropped the case and brought the gun up to his shoulder for three quick shots, tight together, in an attempt at a sudden kill. It failed. The machine rose up unharmed, and a startling clang came back to them as one of the bullets spread itself against a rotor blade and spun off noisily.

The next instant, a barrier of piercing light flowered across the break in front of them as first one, and then two more phosphorus grenades exploded not a dozen feet ahead. An intricate pattern of fern-like structures leapt into the air, dazzlingly etched in pure white smoke, and the vituperative hissing of chemical discharge pitched back at them from the enclosing walls of stalks.

'Round the side—we can't go through—it clings like a bastard!'

MacConnachie plunged into the new field at his right, aiming to work his way round the furious active area of phosphorus, and emerge on the far side of it. Ansell followed. The helicopter was turning back.

As soon as he got among them, MacConnachie saw that the stalks in this field were, in one important respect, different from those in the last: they grew farther apart. This meant that he could run between them much more easily and quickly and that, since his field of vision was correspondingly enlarged, he could watch most of the helicopter's movements most of the time. Also the air was notably clearer, the insects larger and less numerous, the danger of choking much diminished.

As the chopper bore down again, coming this time from their front, he looked up and stopped abruptly. The observer was leaning out of the cabin and aiming some sort of weapon at them. MacConnachie raised his own gun but before he could fire the other man discharged and a bright, glowing red ball flashed into the stalks in front of them. It took MacConnachie so completely by surprise that the observer had withdrawn and the helicopter broken off the contact before he could react.

It was a Very light, fired from a Very pistol. The pilot intended to set this part of the field ablaze as well. The stalks caught at once, flames spurting out from the furiously igniting centre of the conflagration. MacConnachie swung about.

'Back to the break! We'll operate from there!'

As he emerged again into the corridor, turning his face away from the hissing phosphorus, Ansell looked along the fire-break to his left and saw the leading members of the patrol rounding the bend into view. At the same instant they saw him, and aligned their weapons to fire.

'Down, Mac!'

He pitched himself violently backwards into the stalks, taking MacConnachie down with him. A burst of rapid fire slapped and tore at the mushy strip in front of them.

MacConnachie was sure the Goons weren't trying to kill them; they would have been ordered to take them alive. He scrambled up, stepped out into the corridor and fired three carefully aimed shots. Two men went down, the third ran for cover.

The far field was deeply ravaged now, with a tall wall of fire racing towards them; the phosphorus raged blindingly, and the new conflagration set off by the observer was beginning to bite and spread.

'Come on! We haven't any choice!'

They ran into the second half of the field. The race against time and fire was on with a vengeance now. But at least the ground favoured them very slightly: the deeper they committed themselves, the more the stalks thinned out—not dangerously, but enough to provide narrow, roughly uniform corridors down which they could run at full tilt.

But there was still the helicopter.

For some moments MacConnachie was puzzled by its behaviour, for, far from pegging them tight, it began to describe a circle too wide to give any but an approximate idea of their position to the pursuers on the ground. Then he saw another glowing fireball shoot down from the aircraft to bury itself in the field to their right, and he understood. The pilot intended to surround them with a ring of fire.

By now they were running flat out, swishing through the stalks as fast as their legs would carry them, the field having become for them both a series of blurred impressions rushing past on either side and instantly snatched away. The blood roared in their ears, drowning all but the most penetrating sounds, as of a sudden outbreak of unexplained shooting to their right.

When he saw the second light fall MacConnachie jinked left, Ansell stumbling after him. The helicopter curled round behind them and, coming up to pass over their left-hand quarter, discharged another flare into the dried-out stalks. This one was closer and as they ran on they heard the flames begin to crackle and bite. MacConnachie continued his bias to the left but the pilot, completing his manoeuvre, flew across their front, and the observer laid his fourth incendiary directly in their path, thirty yards ahead.

MacConnachie ran straight at it, extending his legs even farther, conscious of Ansell gasping and thudding to his rear. He knew that their best chance to escape the first ring of fire was to pass this flare before it could take and spread to the flares on his right. Already, from that direction, he could see smoke and flames reaching fiercely into the sky.

As he approached it, the ground yawing and pitching in his field of vision, he saw that the flames had crossed the natural path down which they fled, and were already hungrily devouring the file of stalks to his right. But the fire came rushing to meet him so rapidly that, without thought, he lowered his head and plunged through it. In an instant they were on the other side, with barely time to suffer the intense heat before they had left it. At their backs, the flames soared up in a sudden gust of wind to seal the gap through which they had escaped, towering over them, leaning like a building about to fall and crush them.

Again it was necessary to accelerate and, as Ansell flogged himself to keep pace with MacConnachie, the returning pressure of panic forced itself up in his throat, halving what little air his gaping mouth could capture. They had run for many minutes without pause, and there seemed no escape from their predicament: either they would surrender, or they would be burned to death. His whole body pulsated in sympathy with his wrenching heart and, although it was the running that was breaking him, he was only distantly and dizzily aware of this activity. Some part of him inside was about to rupture explosively.

Slack-kneed and flagging, MacConnachie watched the helicopter through a haze of discomfort and strain, cursing uselessly at the frustration of their position. He was coming to a stop, they would have to recover their breath and their wits. There must be a way out, there must be.

Neatly and methodically, the pilot and navigator were sowing a fresh line of incendiaries across their front, but this time far enough distant that MacConnachie could not hope to reach them before they had taken a thorough hold in depth. Even in the time it took him and Ansell to travel another thirty feet, the thin, swirling smoke had sprung all across their front. He came to a stop, gasping, 'You bastard! Oh, you bloody bastard!'

Ansell ran straight into him, and they crashed together to the ground.

For some moments they lay as they had fallen: MacConnachie half-supported by his arms as though unwilling, even in this extremity, to adopt a posture of complete exhaustion; Ansell collapsed across his legs, their bodies whooping with the involuntary, racked undulations of landed fish. Then MacConnachie began to fight back in blind anger, crushing his own body into submission to his will, wrenching Ansell's into a sitting position.

'Sit up! Sit up, damn you!'

Ansell's head flopped about, his neck corded with strain, the breath rushing in and out tormentedly between his clenched teeth.

' 'm all right ... A'righ ... '

But when MacConnachie released him, he began to teeter back and, renewing his grip more firmly on the front of Ansell's native coat, MacConnachie shook him again until the teeth parted in complaint and clashed together.

'Sit—up—damn—you—will—you—sit—up!'

' 'kay—'kay!'

Ansell, face shocked and dazed, put his hands down on MacConnachie's arms to restrain him and, when this support was removed, continued the gesture until, fumblingly, he touched the earth. But he remained upright under his own power.

Deriving his strength now from fury rather than any other source, MacConnachie pushed himself into a standing position and looked about, swaying with fatigue. The sky was dark with hurrying smoke that swept past above the tips of the stalks, and, for the first time, as well as hearing the peculiar moaning of the flames, he could feel the waves of heat that preceded the inferno. Time was desperately short. He sought a glimpse of the helicopter in all the murk, and finally caught sight of it: away to the right, as though he were a child composedly finishing an essay by dotting his 'i's and crossing his 't's, the navigator was neatly sealing off the right flank. Once he had done that, he would turn to the left, and the ring of fire would be complete.

'Come on!'

Without looking back, MacConnachie grabbed the suitcase and gun, and set out as fast as he could for the left flank.

The sounds of the fire were everywhere now, roaring around them, and wherever they looked, except to the left, the pale barriers were writhing across the fields towards them. MacConnachie was dimly aware that there was an exception to this: the last complete barrier laid down, the one across their front, was moving *away* from them, since the general tendency of the fire was to move towards the river. But he didn't see how this could be turned to their advantage. If they tried to follow this front wall out of the field, they would be caught by the back wall rolling up the field behind them.

Anyway, he concluded as he ran, there was still a chance of squeezing out through the left flank.

And then, in seconds, this hope was taken from them. The helicopter came across, four Very lights were discharged into the field, and the last fire-free area was ablaze.

MacConnachie hesitated for a moment then, barely breaking his stride, shouted back to Ansell,

'Run like hell! We're going through!'

There was a chance. The stalks were catching rapidly, but the flares had fallen only a hundred yards ahead. If they could get there quickly enough, the flames would be high but not deep.

Even as he strove hopelessly to extract additional speed from his floundering body, Ansell knew they would never make it. He kept repeating to himself: 'A man can run the hundred yards in 9·2 seconds; a man can run the hundred yards in 9·2 seconds.'

I think it's 9·2.

But the flames leapt up with terrifying speed, skipping from stalk to stalk across their front, and as he peered past MacConnachie's weaving body, desperately anxious now for a clear view of every detail of what lay ahead, the conviction grew in him that to plunge into the fire was to commit suicide. They were getting there far too slowly. It was beyond their stunted capacity.

Then he saw that the helicopter had turned back and was sowing a second barrier beyond the first, and he remembered the endless lines of fields they had seen before ever they committed themselves to the stalks, and he knew for certain that they were nowhere near the edge of the field, and that no escape lay in this direction. His brain shrieked, 'We can't make it, Mac, we can't make it!' and, although he didn't know it, his voice took up the cry:

'We can't make it, Mac!'

Just for a moment he wondered whether MacConnachie meant to kill them both, and then he saw the big man stagger and veer away to the right, and they began to run along the growing wall of fire, heading again towards the river, in a desperate bid to beat the spread of the flames to the far barrier. There was just a chance that they might reach the gap in the top left-hand corner of the field before the two walls joined and became one.

They didn't. They came nowhere near doing so. By the time

they got there, there was no sign that the two fires had ever existed as separate entities. A solid wall of flames raged and swayed in front of them, and as they turned slowly in a complete circle, they saw no gap anywhere.

The fire behind rolled slowly up the field towards them; MacConnachie gave it ten minutes, no more.

Then the helicopter came and sat above them, waiting.

It's odd, thought Ansell, how calm you feel at the moment of realization. If he tells me to fight, I'll fight. If he tells me to die, I'll die. But I won't surrender.

The smoke swept down towards them and fled past overhead, to be lost abruptly in the uprush of flame so close at hand. He didn't feel uncomfortably hot, but the sun was well up in the sky now, and their clothes were oily with sweat; he disliked the smell that issued from the neck of his native coat.

MacConnachie looked up at the helicopter, which hovered thoughtfully just sufficiently distant to avoid troubling them with its turbulence, and contemplated a proposition he had deliberately driven from his mind hitherto: do we surrender, or don't we? Is that what the boy would want? If we do, we'll be kindly treated, that's the Goons' way. But we'll not be ourselves any more. We'll have been defeated.

He turned to the boy.

'Well?'
'Whatever you say, Mac. I'm not bothered.'

That's a big help.

MacConnachie looked at the chopper again. In sudden anger, he brought up the gun and fired three shots at the rotor. It was a waste of time, but it was an answer; or a way of not answering, perhaps.

The helicopter rose up a few feet, then came gently to settle again, waiting. Ansell smiled. Good psychology. Be brave now, but let's see you in five minutes.

MacConnachie said, 'That was stupid.'

Silence; then MacConnachie turned to him, scowling.

'So what do we do? I'm not just standing here.'

'I don't know what we can do, quite honestly.'

'Well, use your bloody brains—that's what you're here for, isn't it?'

'Is it?'

MacConnachie turned away, muttering bitterly,

'Might as well ... doing.'

'What?'

MacConnachie swung back and shouted,

'Might as well be on my own, the good you're doing!'

'What do you expect—a bloody miracle?'

'Yes! Yes! How do we get out of here?'

Again Ansell was filled with the terrible feeling that he had let MacConnachie down, as though he were expected, like some species of god, to intervene only at such times as MacConnachie's own courage and ingenuity were unavailing. Doubtfully, he said,

'Could we take over the chopper?'

'What?'

'Perhaps we could whistle it down and take it over.'

'Can you fly the bastard?'

'No.'

'Neither can I, so that's shit that!'

'For God's sake ... '

'Be some bloody use, why don't you? I *trusted* you! You're the brains!'

'I'm sorry I've been such a nuisance so far!'

'Get stuffed!'

To Ansell there was something grotesque and, for the first time, deeply hopeless about this mean little argument in the midst of such danger; it was almost as though, by its very meanness, it ought in some way to diminish the threat that they faced, but it didn't. MacConnachie turned to him with a look of the utmost disenchantment and reproach.

'We might as well try to follow the front wall out. Come on.'

As he turned and began to walk towards the forward wall of fire, the one that moved so slowly away from them, MacConnachie looked, as he had sounded, at last defeated. Ansell called after him, 'I'm sorry, Mac!'

And then he started to follow.

'There's nothing I can do.'

They trudged in file, ignoring the helicopter, the situation and one another. At their backs, the flames roared up in a fresh gust of wind, and the heat rolled down over them. The volume of sound was immense, a vast moaning and roaring and crackling, so loud that even the buzz of the helicopter came only intermittently to their ears.

When he looked back, Ansell was appalled by the size and rate of progress of the wall of fire. It was creeping forward to left and right and little faster than at the centre, which somehow made the spectacle more horrifying; and the flames reached all of thirty feet into the air, the heat so intense that it was only after another ten feet of rushing vapour that smoke formed and swirled down towards them. It looked to be a horrible death, and yet he found that he could face it. It was the smaller, more personal inconveniences that distressed him: the heat, the smell, the noise, the sense of oppression.

By the time they reached the scorched and ragged edge, where the flares had fallen to set the forward wall on the move, the press of heat had become constant and breathing was difficult. Sweat poured from them. The back wall was no more than four minutes away.

The helicopter had started to behave as though panic had seized its occupants, repeatedly coming right down low as though to remind them that, once they had indicated their surrender, it would need time to land and take them off. MacConnachie smiled. That man should know, if any man did, that surrender was out of the question.

And then the helicopter rose to settle forty feet feet above, waiting for the end, and MacConnachie raised his hand in acknowledgement. The pilot had a clear duty, all else failing, to kill them rather than let them choose their own death; but he, too, raised a hand in salute, and the compact was made.

The moment they stepped on to the smouldering refuse of stalks in an effort to edge closer to the wall of flame before them, Ansell knew they were finished. The heat that came up from the blackened earth was staggering, making him gasp for breath and screw up his whole face in an attempt to escape the scathing radiation behind a shield of his raised arms. In front, through slitted eyes, he saw the figure of MacConnachie picking his way as though he walked on eggshell, the case in one hand, the gun still in the other; it was difficult to make him out properly against the swaying flames beyond.

Now Ansell was afraid, his legs trembled. It was the size of the thing, his inability to make the smallest act that could affect the outcome; he felt hopelessly abandoned, like a child at the mercy of vast, impersonal, adult concerns. The heat possessed him. He could have cried without the least embarrassment.

MacConnachie knew he had been right. The heat was so intense that, when the back wall reached the scorched area, the flames would leap forward to join the front wall without the need of any intervening combustible material; they would be snuffed out just like that.

He couldn't accept it. Nor would he. Outrage and grief forced an odd cry from his lips, and he turned to the boy for one last time.

Against a shimmering background of fire, Ansell saw Mac-Connachie's face. It was covered in scratches and blood.

'Tell me! Tell me! What—to—do!'

Ansell knew it wasn't fear; tears ran down MacConnachie's cheeks, but he wasn't afraid. Ansell began to cry.

'I don't *know*!'

MacConnachie let out a grunt, then struck him in the face with the gun—not hard enough to knock him over, but painfully on the cheek-bone, a crude and yet refined blow. In shock, for an instant, Ansell saw clearly. There was thinner smoke, or paler smoke, behind MacConnachie. And something important was floating out of MacConnachie's forehead.

'Tell me!'

As MacConnachie raised the gun to strike again, Ansell re-focused in the panic of a self-protective reflex, and saw the black dots wheeling in the sky beyond MacConnachie's garish head.

'There! Up there!'

But when MacConnachie turned, the writhing streaks of smoke were swirled together to shut off his view and Ansell let out a little cry of pain at the unfairness of it. Then the smudges whirled apart and the sky was visible again.

'You see!'

'They're shite hawks, that's all.'

'There's water! They circle over water!'

MacConnachie looked again with a growing sense of hope—to the birds, the ground, the birds, the ground. Forty yards. Maybe less. To the point over which the birds are circling. Can't be the river. What is it? Who cares? Forty yards.

Ansell was shouting,

'Come on, Mac! There's water!'

'Wait!' He seized Ansell's coat, restraining him, peering in the smoke for a sight of the chopper. He said firmly, 'We wait.'

And then Ansell lowered his head, and MacConnachie knew that he had seen what MacConnachie himself had appreciated from the first: whatever the water, it lay on the far side of the raging left-hand wall. Ansell mourned.

'Oh God, how can we reach it? How can we ever reach it?'

MacConnachie loosened his grip on Ansell's coat and began absent-mindedly to stroke the back of Ansell's head and neck.

'We'll reach it. Don't worry, we'll get there.'

His mind was on another problem.

The canopy of rushing smoke above their heads was getting thicker and thicker as the flames approached. It must be increasingly difficult, MacConnachie thought, for the pilot to keep track of us; if we wait until the very last and then run into the fire, they may lose us altogether. They might even think we're dead. Of course if we don't get through, we shall be. He watched the back wall of flames, waiting, calculating.

After a moment or two, he became aware that he was standing close to Ansell, touching him. He dropped his arm, and Ansell turned away. MacConnachie couldn't remember tucking the case under his gun arm, but now he returned it to its proper hand. The din was so fierce that he had to shout, and this imparted to his words a note of desperation that annoyed him.

'We wait! At the last minute, run towards the birds! With luck, we'll lose the chopper!'

Ansell turned, quite composed, and nodded. Then he touched his cheek where MacConnachie had struck him, and looked at the left-hand wall. MacConnachie shouted,

'You go first; I follow. When I say!'

Again, Ansell nodded.

Ansell looked at the flames into which they were about to plunge. They would hit the left-hand wall some twenty feet back from its point of conjunction with the front wall. It was a calculated risk. If they hit the wall fast enough, and could keep going long enough, they should come to water. The one factor that favoured them was the tendency of the fire to travel towards the river, thus encouraging forward rather than lateral spread. With luck, the left-hand wall might be as little as fifteen feet deep. But it could be very much more.

He crouched to give himself maximum spring-off. They had a run-up of twenty-five feet. He found that fear had been replaced by lassitude; that his interest in his body's reactions, when he could arouse it, was greater than his terror of them. Dimly he was aware that MacConnachie had crouched beside him.

The back wall came closer, moving faster and faster, the flames leaping and cascading into the sky, sparks showering, the whole structure leaning and twisting, bending and moaning in a vast sheet of destructiveness. The sound was stunning, roaring, rushing upwards, folding over and around them. The air shimmered and stung, hurled about disorderly as it was, and the earth shuddered beneath their feet. Breathing became more and more difficult, the stuff they swallowed harsh and abrasive, hot and scouring. But still MacConnachie delayed, and Ansell trembled in the threat of overbalance. The smoke whipped, and spun, and whirled about them in darting confusion.

'Now!'

First one and then the other, they ran into the raging fire, and flames came together behind them.

For the first six or seven seconds nothing happened. They ran easily, lightly, rushing through the fire, untouched by pain. Then the flames began to bite, and the vicious sting of heat got through to them. First their throats and nostrils seized up, excoriatingly dry, as flesh clung fast to flesh and they creaked open-mouthed. The bottoms of their noses and their cheeks seemed to have been scraped suddenly raw, and raged as though salt were being rubbed into the wounds. They ran on, lashing their bodies to the limit in a screeching rush of sound and raging fire. Smoke sprang from their hair to be sucked instantly away, and their eyelashes shrivelled. All sweat had evaporated, their clothes took on the smudged outline of dissolution. Ansell was screaming, Mac-Connachie cooed oddly. Saliva had no time to form before it was boiled away. The effect was of being flayed alive, each nerve and vein and sinew laid bare to the scorching air. Ansell staggered, foundered dully, his shape losing definition, crumbling into a smouldering presence. The other moving thing that was Mac-Connachie crashed against him, gathered him up, and the combined creature blundered on, smoking. There was a smell of burning meat.

The earth gave way, and they fell through the green scum of many years, releasing a great gout of putrid gases, and screaming and thrashing as the pain hit them.

For many moments, they were properly conscious of nothing but pain, as water bit into raw flesh, and their bodies pitched and twisted to escape this further outrage. Then it was distantly but urgently borne in on MacConnachie, in a renewed access of heat, that the ordeal by fire was not yet ended; from some direction it came at them again.

In an agony of scorched and gasping distress, he peered about him to see what they had fallen into. It was an irrigation ditch or canal of some kind, six to eight feet deep, with four feet of scum-thick water in the bottom. The whole was rough-hewn as a trench and gave every indication of having lain, before their arrival, undisturbed for many years. Wherever he looked, across the surface of the water, which it hid, and up the sides, there lay a rich carpet of dank, proliferating growth, culminating in an outbreak of clinging creepers that had forced their way upwards with groping tendrils to establish a stranglehold among the stalks of the fields above. The trench was deeply shaded and rank. In normal circumstances, it might have been cool.

He found that he and Ansell sat facing one another, with the carpet spread about them at the level of their chests. Ansell's face was drawn fine in suffering. Every now and then he retched, depositing a small quantity of viscous fluid on the surface of the slime. It was only where their abrupt descent had ruptured the fibrous growth that water showed. It was black and still; clearly it had no running source, and was never refreshed by anything but rain. From the entire tacky ooze there issued, in pungent waves, the appalling and pervasive stench of permanent stagnation.

He could not for the moment move. His face raged rawly and, as it did for Ansell, the sickness rose up in him again and again. Oddly enough—for Ansell's pain could hardly be less than his own—it seemed to him that Ansell looked not so much damaged as comic: there was more hair at the bottom of his face than the top, he lacked eyebrows and lashes, and his crown was neatly encased in a skull-cap of green algae. MacConnachie supposed he must look the same. He leaned forward and wiped the filth from the top of Ansell's head and then from his own. Close at hand the suitcase sat sluggish amid the surface weed.

Remembering that he still clutched the gun, he heaved it up and held it before him. It came free from the glutinous mire richly clotted with every variety of muck from bright green to jet black. That needs cleaning, he thought, and wiped it vaguely across his chest; but the sense of urgency had left him, only the memory remained.

Finally he made the attempt to rise and, moving with the suspended caution of an animal that although skinned is living yet, stretched every nerve and muscle to reach the bank on his left.

Twice, unable to lift his feet clear of the coarse mat of vegetation, he fell full length. His outstretched hands pierced the scum, the gun was plunged once more into the black deeps of the trench, and his chest, coming flatly into contact with the spongy substance, was buoyed up for a moment to set the whole surface-area into slow undulation, before the shreds parted and the water seeped through to meet him. With every movement he released more of the vile, poisonous gases.

By the time he reached the bank, floundering and heaving and choking on his own smell, there was nothing to separate the gun from his arm, or the man from the swamp. He was loaded down with filth and so uncertain of his balance that he let the gun fall, reached up to the nearest stalks, and hung there recuperating.

Coherence had returned to Ansell less quickly but more demoralizingly. As the worst of his nausea subsided and the pain became more embraceable, he had been betrayed by his imagination. He sat now quite rigid, afraid to move, suffering one of those moments of paralysing doubt, familiar from childhood, in which the mind knows that something terrible has happened to the body and refuses to acknowledge it. So long as he remained absolutely still, he could not drop apart.

The beginnings of urgency had returned to MacConnachie. They could not stay here; he must orient himself. He laid his head back and looked at the sky. Thin billows of smoke puffed out occasionally over their hiding-place, but were driven at once towards the river. So the river was down there, and he clung in fact to the right-hand bank of the trench. But smoke was coming also from behind him. He arched right back, hanging from the stalks, to peer into the sky above the left-hand side of the trench. Yes, there was another fire, coming fast but not yet level with the ditch. How did it get there?

He shook his body in an anguished attempt to think. Of course, it was the second layer of incendiaries the pilot had put down out-side the left-hand wall of the burning field. The pilot would be a hard man to convince. He would want to see remains. But could he reasonably expect to after so raging an inferno? Yes. *I* would.

Ignore the pain, think some more. The Goons have got a tiger by the tail. If they can't put out the fire, it will destroy the village. So if they think we're dead ...

It was no good. He had to rest. He lowered his face for a mo-ment into the relatively cool sludge of the bank. Then he groped for and found the gun, turned up the bottom edge of his native coat, and tried to find a cleaner patch with which to wipe it. It made little difference, but at least the weapon took on the approximate outline of a firearm.

He looked again at Ansell, screwing up his eyes with the effort of concentration, and setting the stinging rawness of his face throbbing and jangling once more. The stench was suffocating, making him cough; if they didn't get out of this place soon, they'd be gassed to death.

Ansell looked curiously calm, sitting among the weeds like a man in a bubble bath, his eyes cast in the thoughtful and distant aspect of a day-dreamer.

'Kid!'

Silence.

'Kid—wake up!'

Ansell didn't seem to hear him. What was strange was that MacConnachie couldn't hear himself, except at the muted and disturbing level of a man with damaged eardrums. Alarmed, he stuffed the gun up among the creepers, and put his hand to his ears; then, having diagnosed the trouble, he chuckled as he gouged the muck out of them.

The boy was less than six feet away, but if MacConnachie relinquished the support of the bank he'd be down in the dross again for sure. So, taking a firm hold on a stalk with one hand, he extended his body as far as it would stretch, reaching out towards Ansell with the other. His fingers remained a few inches short of Ansell's face. He waved his arm about and shouted, 'Ansell! Wake up! Snap out of it!'

Ansell didn't, and MacConnachie was causing himself wrenching agony. He lowered a foot into the filth and kicked some of it up at Ansell's face. The boy turned to look at him with an expression of puzzlement and fear. MacConnachie renewed his gestures, shouting louder, hurting himself.

In MacConnachie's face, Ansell saw his own, and it gave him hope. The eyebrows were gone, the lashes and most of the hair. The ears protruded startlingly, a glowing red at their extremities. All of the face was burnt bright red, the sides of the neck as well, and the eyes were deep hollows of shock. But his friend was moving, his mouth opened and shut. He still had a full complement of facial skin, the bones were nowhere visible, and that was an arm. He even had a nose to his credit.

As his eyes travelled downwards, Ansell thought, how did he get so dirty? Then he saw that MacConnachie was shouting and gesticulating. He tried very hard to catch the words, but something had happened to his ears. He was stone deaf.

'For Christ's sake clean your ears out!'

Recognition was coming slowly into the boy's eyes.

'Your ears, man—your ears!'

MacConnachie plunged a finger back into one of his own ears, waggling it about by way of demonstration. Ansell imitated him and said,

'What did you say?'

MacConnachie burst into irresistible laughter at the forlornness of it, wrenching his face painfully again.

'How do you feel?'

'Sick and sore.'

'So do I. Come over here.'

Then, as Ansell put down his hands to lever himself up, apparently surprised to see the swamp, MacConnachie added, 'Carefully!'

Ansell stood up, the strap of the canteen pulled tight about his neck, the weight reasserted itself, and he disappeared face down into the filth. Again MacConnachie roared with laughter.

'Oh God, what's the use?' He released the stalk resignedly and stepped forwards, reaching out with his arms. 'Come on, kid.'

As Ansell came up spluttering and vomiting, smeared now from head to foot with clotted slime, he made a wild grab at MacConnachie and they both went down. MacConnachie couldn't stop laughing, it rose up in him irrepressibly.

'Jesus God!'

He seized the nearest part of Ansell, which happened to be his chest, and heaved him over to the bank. But Ansell, with no chance to take hold of anything, simply cannoned off it and, as MacConnachie skidded after him through the squishy muck at the bottom of the trench, fell back on top of him again.

MacConnachie surfaced screaming comically.

'For Christ's sake, stand up!'

He took hold of Ansell in farcical desperation, turned him about, pinned him to the bank, then, seizing one hand, clamped it firmly round a stalk. At which, his balance exhausted, he fell back to sit with a tremendous crash and a gout of spume, once more encased in the vile ordure of the ditch but still laughing. Ansell stayed upright.

The newly released stench was appalling, the surface of the mire only slowly settling to rest, the suitcase bobbing heavily. He reached for it, dragged it with him to the bank, and somehow got it wedged with the gun among the creepers above. Then he embraced Ansell from behind, holding with his longer arms to more distant stalks, supporting the boy with his own body and resting against him.

'How do you feel?'

MacConnachie's lips were close to his ear.

'Not too bad.'

In fact his face hurt so that he could weep, but the sickness, surprisingly, had left him, and the repulsive dross with which he was smeared and the choking stench had diminished to manageable proportions. He was grateful for MacConnachie's aid, so immediately and unthinkingly given, but now that the worst of his need had subsided, he felt a different compulsion: to reassert himself. He said,

'What now?'

MacConnachie understood at once: the boy was strong enough to stand alone, and wanted to. He edged along, still gripping the stalks, until he stood beside him. He spat the muck out of his mouth and looked at the sky.

'We'll have to move, towards the river.'

'Do you think we convinced them we're dead?'

'I don't know about them, but I bloody near convinced myself.'

'I can hear the chopper.'

With ears unclogged and senses more about them, they became aware of sound again. The roar of the fire continued unabated, though muted now by the walls of the depression in which they stood. The sound of the helicopter's engine, roaring at one moment, at another distantly whining, came through persistently in nagging counterpoint.

'He's quartering the field,' MacConnachie said.

And looking for us, he thought. He's meant to be directing the fire-fighters, but that man's having a damned good look for for us. We'll have to wait till the smoke gets thicker.

131

'As soon as the flames get really close, we'll go out the left-hand side.'

'Across the front of that second fire?'

'Yes.'

Ansell had seen it: it was clearly the danger now. Already, as well as being putrid, the air was stiflingly hot. He turned his face away, and looked down the trench in the direction of the river. It came to an abrupt end fifteen feet away. He said to MacConnachie,

'Is that any use?'

'What?'

He indicated that at the far end there stood in slime the ruin of an ancient monsoon drain, its stone arch cracked and crumbling, its weathered feet sunk deep and darkly stained with green and black corruption. Within, they saw the mouth of a dank, narrow cavern.

'What for?'

'To hide in.'

'Kid, this whole place will boil when the fire comes. I don't think we could take another roasting. We're done to a turn already.'

'Then shouldn't we find somewhere to lie up till night?'

'No, they're more worried about the fire than us.'

Ansell doubted this, but felt too tired to argue. He looked into the sky.

'Hey, Mac, look!'

'The shite hawks.'

'But why are they up there? Is it the tributary?'

'Yes. Yes, it is.'

And now MacConnachie knew exactly where they were. The burning field was on their right. The river ran across their front. To their left and behind was the second fire. To their left and in front was the small tributary that curled back on itself, the one he had seen from the hills before they entered the valley. The birds, of course, had always been wheeling over that, but he had misjudged the distance and chance had led them to the ditch.

The tributary was still fifty yards distant; it would serve as their first objective.

Suddenly there was an outbreak of shouting to their right, answered at once by calls from the left. Ansell said,

'They're all around us.'

'They have been all the time. They're nearer now, that's all.'

The helicopter roared close again, momentarily blotting out the raging crackle of the fire, but it failed to appear in the sky above them, and shortly afterwards faded to its lower register.

'That man doesn't believe we're dead, does he?'

'Kid, you're learning. We'll head for the tributary. Check gear, then move.'

They went rapidly through their possessions; nothing was missing. MacConnachie took the suitcase and gun, Ansell the canteen and knife, and they plunged into the filth once more.

At the far bank, gasping, they rested. Then MacConnachie hauled himself clear at the second attempt, reached down to help Ansell, and they were back among the stalks again.

MacConnachie was happy to be on their true line of march once more. Looking to the birds for guidance, he led the way at a crouching lope towards the tributary. But the stalks, he noticed, grew thinner all the time, and he was oppressed by the fact that they found themselves constantly looking down long corridors of neat sticks, from the far end of which they might be spotted at any moment. With a grunt he stopped, raised a finger to his lips for silence, and cleaned the gun as best he could with the muck-blackened tail of his coat. Moving on, he made no attempt at speed; now that contact was broken again, and the initiative within their grasp, he did not intend to relinquish dominance through carelessness. Every time a shout arose, which happened often, he paused, waiting for silence, before pressing on. Then, halfway to the tributary, he entered a corridor and froze.

Looking over MacConnachie's shoulder, absolutely still, Ansell saw that one of the three-man patrols was walking towards them from the other end, its members jabbering to one another and pointing through the stalks towards the fire. Mac-Connachie was inching the weapon up into a firing position. The Goons were shouting loudly, rather excitedly, as though the day had come as an adventure to break their dull military routine. Ansell noticed, for the first time in many hours, how hot the sun was.

Abruptly the Goons turned off in answer to a shout that arose from startlingly close at hand, and disappeared behind the screen of stalks towards the fire. Ansell had not realized the ring was so tight about them. He waited, sweating, for MacConnachie to start again, but they had only gone ten yards when the second patrol came into view, trudging through the stalks, kicking in sweaty anger and cursing dully; and even before this group had passed, a third could be heard coming very close.

MacConnachie flattened himself to spring, Ansell doing the same. But the stalks parted suddenly six feet ahead, and the Goons stamped across without looking at them. By now they could hear yet more patrols approaching. Some sort of general call must have gone out; this part of the field was alive with groups of men moving towards the fire.

They fell into a tense and desperate game of hide-and-seek, advancing a few yards, hiding to let a patrol pass through, advancing and hiding again; but all the time they worked their way closer to their objective.

They reached it before the knew they were upon it; Mac-Connachie parted some stalks, leant through, and from the angle at which his feet rose up Ansell realized that he was teetering forward suddenly without support. He threw himself down on MacConnachie's legs to provide a counterbalance.

MacConnachie was hanging, head down, over a stream of relatively clear water. He twisted back and whispered urgently, 'Take the gun!'

Ansell reached down awkwardly for it. Then MacConnachie said, 'Let me go!'

Ansell raised his weight, MacConnachie dropped the suitcase and slid after it into the water. At once he came to his feet, handed the suitcase up to Ansell, and looked about him.

It was possible to see for nearly fifty feet along the tributary before it turned off on its twisted course to the river; the stalks grew right up to the banks on either side. There was little smoke in the sky and, although the sounds of the fire and the helicopter were still audible, they were distant. No scent of immediate danger came to him and on impulse he rinsed himself and his clothes as quickly and thoroughly as he could; then, taking Ansell's place on the bank, he told him to do the same.

Ansell jumped at the way the water, warm though it was, stung his face; but he washed himself. It had become important that he and MacConnachie should suffer the same degree of pain.

There flowed from him across the yellow surface a skein of dark discoloration; free from the worst of the filth, he felt refreshed.

With Ansell once more crouching at his side, MacConnachie listened and watched. Within the walls of the tributary they would be deaf and blind. He remembered, too, that it turned soon to the left to join the delta; he had decided therefore to travel along its bank until they reached that bend, and then to strike out to the right for the least populated part of the valley where, according to his original plan, they would cross the river.

But a new problem had arisen. It wasn't simply that the numbers of people pushing their way through the stalks had increased, but that he had heard first one woman's voice, and then another, and knew that the villagers had joined the fight to save their crops. MacConnachie hated civilians. To avoid patrols was one thing— the behaviour of trained soldiers was familiar to him—but the 'others' were unpredictable; they mooched and slopped about, they fell asleep and became bored. Women were the worst; a man could fall over them.

With a sigh, he led the way forward.

Until they reached the bend in the tributary, progress was rapid and professional. The clamour to their right increased in variety —he even heard an infant bawl—but he suffered it. Then they had to turn right into the open field.

It was becoming intolerably hot. Ansell suddenly realized that it must be nearly midday, and he was astonished. Until this moment, he had given no thought to the hour. His face felt stiff and dry, as though it had taken on the texture of gauze; he was unwilling to form an expression.

By now the stalks were dangerously thin. Again and again they sighted groups of figures to their right, or leapt startled at the closeness of an unexpected voice; for every yard they moved forward, minutes were spent in an agonized watchfulness as villagers dragged past. They were approaching the open fields, where the stalks would end, and the flat expanses of water-logged clay would lie between themselves and the river. For the life of him, Ansell could not see how MacConnachie intended to cross this hazard with the helicopter still in the sky, and the entire area alive with an alarmed and alert populace.

Then MacConnachie came face to face with the child. He was a boy of about six, with all the wide-eyed expansiveness of his age. His straight black hair hung down in a fringe across his forehead. For some moments, he stared at MacConnachie in astonishment, legs apart, little fists uncoiling in shock. Then his face darkened with uncertainty, and finally lit with growing alarm. Eyes intent on MacConnachie's features, he opened his mouth as if to call out, and Ansell caught the quick movement of Mac-Connachie's gun arm.

My God, he thought, he means to kill him.

But even as he stretched out an arm in restraint, MacConnachie leant forward to ruffle the boy's hair, chuckling, soothing him with a murmur in his own language. The boy's expression softened, as though the familiar words had reassured him; then at last he grinned in response to something MacConnachie said, and Ansell relaxed, appalled to find how tightly he had been holding himself.

With confidence came curiosity. The boy was now clearly demanding an explanation as to why two adults should be down on their knees, at his level, in what he evidently regarded as a private playground. MacConnachie seemed to enjoy explaining. Since Ansell didn't understand the words, he had to deduce their meaning from the changing expressions on the boy's face. It came to him that MacConnachie was describing some sort of complicated game; and that, he thought, would prove to be a mistake. So it did. For the boy wanted to join in. And when MacConnachie attempted to persuade him of the impossibility of this, a crisis of confidence ensued.

Ansell was becoming restless and afraid. Away to their right a growing cloud of smoke was visible, thickened by attempts to damp the fire. Figures passed back and forth beneath it with increasing frequency; it was only a matter of time before someone looked their way and since, although stationary, MacConnachie was obliged to make small movements to communicate with the boy, discovery was an imminent threat. And MacConnachie had fallen into a trap.

In his efforts to quell the child's growing disillusion, Mac-Connachie had apparently offered a gift in place of the game.

Now, as he reached down for pockets that were no longer there, he hesitated, and Ansell knew exactly what was passing through his mind. He had nothing to give. And the boy was a danger, one of the enemy: a pair of eyes and a mouth that had to be closed.

Contact had been re-established.

Ansell found that he was locked in a terrible premonition of impending horror. He was unable to move or to speak; the cast of MacConnachie's neck was riveting, his shoulders hypnotic. The boy was regarding MacConnachie with a steady gaze of anticipation and confidence, his head a little to one side as though to make the blow easy and clean. The voices grew suddenly distant.

MacConnachie reached out and took one of the boy's hands between his thick, dirty fingers as though to prevent him from escaping or as though, by this means, he might draw from that source something of which he was desperately in need. The boy smiled a little; he might at that moment have been much the older of the two.

Then a woman's voice called out in alarm from very close, and Ansell jumped with fright. But MacConnachie, as though to prevent the passage of his own fear to the child, remained very still, holding him. He need not have concerned himself. The boy came upright at once, stepped back, and looked towards the voice with disappointment and doubt. Then he looked at MacConnachie with an expression of regret. MacConnachie reached up and ruffled his hair. Suddenly the boy laughed and wrapped his small brown arms round MacConnachie's neck. MacConnachie held him a moment then, turning him about, sent him running off to his mother with a smack on the bottom. The boy didn't look back. He seemed not to have noticed Ansell at all.

As MacConnachie's face, following the flight of the child, came round towards him, Ansell got his first clear look at it. There was so much uncertainty and doubt therein, such confusion and fear for the consequences of a stupid and impulsive weakness, that Ansell could have wept for his friend at that moment.

Would the boy talk? What was happening to them, that so much depended on the natural urge of a child to share an adventure with his parents?

MacConnachie knew he had made an elementary mistake. A child might be expected to see people in the grass, but not such obvious foreigners. He should have killed the brat. What was the matter with him?

God keep him silent, the little bastard.

And now it went bad on them. A great shout of consternation rose up from the right, and looking they saw a gout of flame spurt up into the sky. A fierce gust of wind set all the stalks chattering, as though God had sneezed. They thought it was the helicopter, but that remained distant, buzzing. All around, the concatenation multiplied with increasing desperation as the smoke thickened.

The sudden stroke of nature seemed to bring MacConnachie to himself, for he pressed forward now with greater urgency, cleaving through the stalks with rapid, professional precision, slipping past stray figures to left and right; but much too fast, Ansell thought, as though, a climax approaching, he must rush forward to embrace the disaster.

In minutes they reached the limits of the stalks and, crouching side by side, looked out over an expanse of unprotected, soggy mud-flat. The huts began only two hundred yards to their left; they had hit too close to the village. Low dykes ran down towards the river, meeting others and breaking out at right angles to contain the rectangular boxes of cultivation. Isolated trees stood at various points but, together with the low walls, they constituted the only cover and were useless. The river was three hundred yards to their front, but they could not reach it. The entire area was animate with dozens of villagers running about in a state of great excitement, chattering among themselves and carrying, Ansell would have said pointlessly, slung paniers of water towards the fire. If they propose to extinguish it by such a method, he thought, we are here for the day.

MacConnachie, still moving with what seemed to Ansell an undue and dangerous haste, made one more attempt to work along the perimeter of stalks to their right, but it was futile. The farther they went in that direction, the greater the number of villagers with whom they were forced to play hide and seek. And by now the thick pall of greasy smoke was drifting down over them, creating the additional hazard of discovery through choking, so difficult had breathing become.

At length MacConnachie stopped and looked slowly all about them, clearly seeking a way out of their dilemma; but there was none. They could go neither forward nor back. They were trapped at the edge of the burning field as the fire drew closer.

For the third time that day, MacConnachie was involved in a crisis of confidence: not this time in Ansell's intelligence or a child's trust, but in his own strange and particular abilities.

To have made the mistake with the child was bad enough, but now he had committed a major tactical blunder. What was the matter with him? Why in the name of God wasn't he *alone*?

The moment Ansell's eyes—not his abilities, but Ansell's eyes—had saved them from the fire, they should have gone to ground. Ansell had told him. Ansell had seen his mistake and warned him: 'Shouldn't we lie up till night?' he had said, and MacConnachie had said 'No.' Now he had thrown the whole lot away.

Ansell said quietly at his side,

'Mac, we must go back to the tributary.'

'Don't be so bloody stupid!'

'The Goons will use it as a fire-break, they can't control the fire. On the other side, we'll be safe.'

It was true. The Goons would have to let the fire burn itself out. That meant they would let it advance to the mud-flats at the front, and on the left-hand side allow it a controlled spread as far as the tributary, where they could contain it. What happened to the right was not MacConnachie's concern. But at any moment a party would be sent to scythe down the stalks on either side of the tributary.

He should have seen all this. In a black mood, hating Ansell, he snarled,

'We'd better bloody hurry then!'

Once across, they wormed deep into the next field, and settled to keep watch; but they fell asleep. Neither slept for long, and when they woke their faces seemed once more to be on fire. Ansell came awake screaming, and MacConnachie was forced to clap a hand over his mouth to silence him. Both then suffered a period of depression and pain, in which the wretchedness of their condition sat heavily upon them. Individually, they found that their facial skin had become distressingly stiff; and each saw, on the other, a faint beading of crystalline seepage to which neither referred. They sat in silence.

MacConnachie produced the remainder of the meat, uneaten from breakfast, and they had an early meal, neither man finding it easy to eat, for they were suffering from shock. Then they drank. It occurred to Ansell, to his astonishment, that he had not felt thirsty after being so badly burned in the field, that he had not even thought of water until this moment. It was remarkable; as though his body had taken on a new and paradoxical set of reactions.

When they squatted, relief came at once, and both gave vent

to their amusement, splitting their faces with laughter. The skin wept.

MacConnachie cleaned the gun, worrying because his hands would not stop trembling. Fear was an old friend, but its outward expression a new enemy.

The Goons came and cut down the stalks beside the tributary. The fire burned until it reached the water, where it died, dying also at the mud-flats. But far to the right it burned as strongly as ever, and was burning still when night came. At last it was their ally, for it drew attention away from them, and stood as a beacon for their night crossing of the valley. The helicopter lingered above the flames but its sting was drawn, darkness and the demands of the fire rendering it impotent. MacConnachie knew it was time to move, and rose. Ansell said, 'Give me the gun.' He took it and handed it back.

'It's still on single-shot.'

MacConnachie snorted softly.

'Come on.'

But it was a necessary touch of warmth in the darkness. Now his hands were steady. It did not occur to him that it was a warning as well; already Ansell's attention to this detail had become haphazard.

There was no moon. They passed the point from which they had turned back and, walking upright, stepped out on to the mud-flats. At their backs the fire raged steadily, distant now, thrusting fingers of flame into the sky, imparting a flickering glow to the air above. All about them rose up the musty odour of fire recently extinct, heavy in the cool, dank night.

They kept close to the shadow of the low walls, but encountered no danger. Once or twice louder noises rose above the gentle murmur of the late evening village, and if they looked to their left they could see the formation of streets in the pattern of the lights. All talk must be of the fire; it represented a vast loss to the community. On one occasion a boat passed slowly down the river, a lamp burning in its stern; this was useful to them since, with no moonlight reflected off the water, it had become difficult to judge how far they had to go.

In fifteen minutes they reached the river line. MacConnachie signalled to Ansell to cover him from the angle of the nearest wall, and advanced to the water's edge. He crouched and looked both ways along it, listening. Then he turned to face inland, lowering himself until his chin touched the earth. By this means he was able to project the nearest features against the skyline; there was nothing to cause alarm: a hut or two, one tree. He turned back to the river and, leaning out over it, lowered his head until his cheek almost touched the water. From this posture he looked again along the river, first one way and then the other, for fully two minutes in each direction. At length, satisfied, he rose, signalled Ansell to rejoin him, and led the way along the river bank to the right. In five minutes they came to a small jetty, dark against the leaden water, where a boat sat sluggishly berthed, tapping gently.

For no reason, Ansell had supposed that the river flowed from right to left. He saw now that the reverse was true, and that happily even the water would help them to maintain their bias to the right.

At MacConnachie's indication he stepped down into the boat, holding firmly to MacConnachie's outstretched arm in case, tilting at the sudden weight, the hulk should precipitate him into the water. There was the danger, too, that the shell might tear under his foot, so powerful was the smell, and alarming the touch, of soft, rotting timber. But the craft held together and MacConnachie joined him, taking the stern position and pushing off, to set the boat in heavy motion across the water. It was a restful progress and Ansell kept thinking, it's too easy, it's too easy.

MacConnachie unshipped the single oar and, settling it over the stern, propelled them forward with cautious sweeps, relying for the most part on the drift of the river to carry them to the farther bank. Ansell turned now and peered over the bows into the gloom, trying to make out some shape at the other side of the river.

Time passed and they drifted gently, little waves slapping softly against the side of the boat in face of a faint breeze. Then Ansell found that he was able to make out the first, larger shapes that lay ahead and realized the next moment that, on their present course, they would arrive directly below the only visible hut. As he turned to warn MacConnachie, a shout rose up from the bank they had just quit.

He froze, his stomach pinched tight again with fear. He could see the dark bulk of MacConnachie as unmoving as himself, the oar suspended a few inches above the water. Silence closed about them, disturbed only by the gentle lapping of the waves and a faint drip from the oar.

Then the shout came again, louder but still questioning. They waited. Out of the corner of his eye, Ansell could see the fire flickering beyond the shadow of MacConnachie's head. He thought he heard a sound behind him and then, or so it seemed to him, the pale diffusion of light increased slightly. MacConnachie muttered,

'Someone on the other bank has lit a lamp. We must be visible in silhouette.'

Ansell couldn't turn his head, for his face was towards the questioning voice, but he assumed it must be the occupant of the hut he had seen. Suddenly the voice commanded angrily; they had been spotted. MacConnachie turned and shouted back, imparting to his tone the slur of drunkenness and laughing raucously. There was a pause, and when the voice replied it seemed to Ansell that he understood every word: 'Why the bloody hell didn't you say so?' MacConnachie called again, more drunk but placatory. There was a brief complaining murmur, and the conversation ended.

But another started: the man with the lamp decided to reactivate the dialogue. MacConnachie stood up and, turning the boat along the flow of the river, shouted back. For some minutes a cheerful conversation ensued, growing louder and louder as man and boat drew farther apart, until at length, with an exchange of mutual good wishes, it too ended. MacConnachie was chuckling softly to himself, obviously stimulated; and now Ansell understood something that, until this moment, he had not perceived: MacConnachie actually *enjoyed* these moments of contact. Perhaps they restored his confidence; perhaps they convinced him that, their disguise intact, they were indeed part of the landscape through which they passed; but Ansell doubted it. He felt there was another reason he didn't altogether understand. Rather crossly, he whispered,

'What was that all about?'

'Us. The Goons are blaming us for the fire. We started it.'

'That *is* charming.'

'Let's get ashore.'

Using the oar as a tiller, MacConnachie pointed the prow of the boat towards the opposite shore, and they drifted in. Just before they hit the bank Ansell leapt up on to it, holding fast to the bow rope. Then MacConnachie scrambled ashore, took the rope, shoved the boat out as far into the water as it would go, and left it to drift gently down the river out of sight. They turned and flattened themselves against the earth, having first advanced a little from the dangers of the water's edge.

There were few huts about; the night was dark; and the worst water hazard was behind them. MacConnachie was pleased. But soon the night glow would come, and they must master the remaining two tributaries before then. There had been nothing to gain by taking the boat with them, since neither tributary was deep or wide, and the disadvantages outweighed the potential gain. Unlike Ansell, he was not troubled by the feeling that things were going too smoothly. Experience had taught him that when luck came, it came a bundle, and the wise man rode it; when it went, it went completely and without warning. He led the way forward.

The first tributary was simplicity itself. They hoisted their possessions, waded across, felt the water rise to the level of their chests then down to their knees again, and climbed out.

The second tributary wasn't like that at all.

Halfway there, MacConnachie was sure he heard a noise to his front. He stopped and they spread to ten feet apart, waiting. No sound came. He could see nothing but ill-defined shapes in the gloom. For fifteen minutes he remained absolutely still, projecting his instincts, confidently at first, and then again and again in an increasingly desperate attempt to absorb the feel of the territory ahead. But it didn't work. For the first time he groped blindly, but no picture came. Fifteen more minutes, sick at heart and chill; but nothing came. They had to move on, but suddenly to be so uncertain, where he was generally so sure, racked him achingly. With nerves stretched unbearably, he floated forward in a state of painfully acute awareness, as though nothing stood between himself and raw apprehension, and the smallest noise, of a beetle crushed, might crash against his inner ear.

They were inching along the side of a hut; to avoid it at this bad moment would be too dangerous. The tributary lay fifteen feet ahead. It might be the building, MacConnachie thought, a presence so oppressive to him, that blunted his perceptions, blocking the signals that normally came through to him.

But once they were clear of it he advanced to the very edge of the water and, lying prone, waited and waited for danger to make itself felt; but none did. Minutes passed. He was in a condition of utter uncertainty; he had no idea what to do. It was as though the gift had suddenly fled from him to a distance; but somewhere, just beyond the rim of its present horizon, an alarm signal clamoured persistently to be let in.

And then the night grew lighter. The glow had come, early, and MacConnachie felt abandoned.

Ansell was shocked by how clearly, all of a sudden, he could make out the shape of MacConnachie against the earth. And he had the tingling feeling that waves of distress were radiating from the other man, which disturbed him greatly. MacConnachie returned with exquisite slowness and deliberation, thrust the gun at him, took the knife and, after much cautious wriggling by Ansell, the canteen, and left the suitcase. His instructions, unspoken, were clear: cover me, I'm going to cross the tributary.

Watching the gliding shadow, Ansell fretted fearfully. Why was MacConnachie so suddenly afraid?

MacConnachie crawled forward and entered the water, lowering himself feet first until he touched the bottom. He found that he had to bend his knees a little to leave only his head above the surface. With the canteen hanging round his neck, and the knife clutched in his right hand at waist level, he waited for a moment or two; then launched himself gently forward.

Although this was the narrowest belt of water they had so far encountered, it flowed not more quickly but more slowly than the others, with a flat, sluggish drift. He had no trouble in staying upright. Foot by foot he worked his way across towards the other bank. He was more than halfway there when a voice spoke. Quite casually, in the Goon language, it said,

'*There's no one there.*'
'*Be quiet.*'
'*I tell you …*'
'*Shut up, Pig Shit!*'

147

Why didn't you warn me, MacConnachie cried in his head, why didn't you warn me? We tried, we tried, said the inner voices, but where were you?

Ansell felt sick with fear. Have they seen him? What are they saying? Keep still, Mac, in Christ's name. I don't know where to shoot. I'm blind.

Now that he had heard them, MacConnachie saw them. Four darker shadows against the lightening sky above the bank; four Goons, four guns. But Christ they were good. One of them was. They had outwaited him. It must be the one who called the other Pig Shit. MacConnachie knew how he felt.

It happened so gradually that Ansell was appalled suddenly to realize that he couldn't see MacConnachie. One moment his head had been there, just visible against the pale water; the next it was gone.

Be careful, Mac.

Oh, God, don't let him die!

Under the water, MacConnachie knew he would have to act quickly. He couldn't breathe out until he was under the lee of the far bank; the bubbles would betray him. He must keep low, move slowly—the weight of the canteen helped there—and he mustn't lose his sense of direction.

He came up against the soft mass of the bank, twisted his head over his shoulder until he faced upwards, then rose slowly, using the canteen as an anchor. First his nose, then his lips and eyes broke the surface. He let out breath in an agonized, silent gasp. He could see little that would orient him: the sky, and the dark edge of the overhang. He breathed deeply for a moment or two, then let himself rise up until his ears and head were clear of the water. His heart beat more steadily. He waited and listened.

Ansell searched the shadowed cut of the far bank again and again, but he could see nothing. He must be there, he told himself. I can only wait.

Time passed: five minutes; ten; fifteen. This Goon was too damned good. MacConnachie was cold. Compared to the night air, the water was warm, but he shivered and trembled all over. He pressed the knife into the flesh of his thigh to diminish the other discomforts. Then a voice, directly above him, said,

'*Maybe you're right. Here.*'

'*Thanks.*'

'*But don't talk on patrol again, or I'll have 'em for door knockers.*'

'*Yes, sir.*'

There was a momentary glow above him, then a match tumbled down to hiss in the water and float past.

'*Keep it shaded.*'

'*Yes, sir.*'

Silence. Bitter cold.

'*The fire is nearly out.*'

'*What a load of dross they are. No guts. No discipline. A rabble.*'

'*They should be in your unit for a week, sir.*'

'*They should truly. In the old days …*'

He's been in the water for more than half an hour, Ansell thought. But he must be safe. There's been no shooting, and they've started to talk again. I must stay awake. I must be ready to move the moment he needs me. My elbows are going to sleep. It won't get any lighter now till dawn. I wish I could see him. I wonder if he can see me? Why don't they *go*?

MacConnachie had been comforted by the lighting of the cigarette. The man was good, he thought, but getting old. Been in a base or training camp too long. Can't take it any more. He'll move soon because he'll have to.

He was good once, though. He'd had it then. It never leaves you completely. They'll learn something, those young soldiers, if they've any brains at all. That man won't die easily.

Cold, cold.

This bloody canteen weighs a ton.

It wasn't until they left that Ansell saw them. He had seen the cigarette being lit, and he knew where they were; but it wasn't until they turned away and headed back towards the village that he was able to make out the four distinct shapes.

Don't move. Wait for Mac. He is relying on you to be in the same place.

MacConnachie saw the cigarette fall into the water, and heard them go away but, chilled to the bone though he was, he spent another ten minutes immersed in the tributary. Should have been fifteen. Must be getting old. But we've already lost an hour.

Ansell felt an immense surge of relief as he saw the dark shape haul itself from the water. For the first time he discovered how stiff and cold he had become. Setting the gun and suitcase ready, he waited eagerly for MacConnachie to signal. He saw Mac-Connachie look about, select a position from which he would be silhouetted against the sky to a man in Ansell's position, and make the recognized gesture of Come To Me.

Ansell went.

Crouching beside MacConnachie, Ansell saw that the older man was shivering badly, every now and then releasing a slight, involuntary grunt. Having just passed through the tributary himself, and with his wet clothes chill against his legs, he realized how wearing and destructive the vigil in the water must have been. He knew that they must move at once, to restore the older man's circulation.

'I'll take the lead,' he whispered, and MacConnachie nodded at once.

Ansell slid forward, gun at the ready, suitcase in his other hand. MacConnachie followed with the canteen and the knife.

Now that the glow had come, Ansell was able to rely on his eyes rather than MacConnachie's instinct, which he himself lacked. The shadows were yet darker, but the general configuration easier to make out. He saw a patrol and, halting MacConnachie, lay up until it had passed from view. But they made good time, and twenty minutes brought them to the edge of the outgoing mud-flats.

MacConnachie came up, exchanged canteen and knife for suitcase and gun, and once more took over the lead.

They went up the side of a retaining dyke. Near a single tree MacConnachie sensed danger, and drew Ansell into a crouch beside him. A patrol emerged to the right, clearly visible against the dull mirror of the mud. Its members wandered about for some moments, peering this way and that, but finally they peeled off in file to disappear in the direction of the tributary. Still MacConnachie kept a restraining hand on Ansell's arm, and five minutes later another patrol came into view. This group moved purposefully across the mud-flats in extended order until they passed out of their field of vision to the left.

MacConnachie had *sensed* them; he had *known* they were coming. He glowed inside with all the pleasure of a child discovering that the lost Teddy bear is found. The gift had come back to him.

He knew there was no more danger to their front. In forty minutes they reached the foot of the mountain range, where the slopes rose sheer as cliffs dropping into a sea. They started to climb out of the valley, his first objective at last achieved; but it would be at least another thirty hours before they had done with the valley, or the valley had done with them.

For tomorrow they would have to return.

Once again, the ground over which they travelled had changed character entirely. Here it was all angles, edges and spars, the gradient vastly steeper than the relative undulations of the hill range. To scale the mountains at all was going to be a punishing experience in their weakened condition; Ansell found even the early slopes witheringly destructive. But he stayed close behind MacConnachie until nearly four when the older man called a halt and, with nothing left of the day's rations to eat, they fell into an exhausted sleep.

The sixth day. The dawn failed to wake MacConnachie, but the helicopter did.

He opened his eyes, not otherwise moving. He could see nothing but sky. He rotated his eyes to take in the fullest possible field of view, but still he saw nothing but sky and the upper rim of the depression in which they lay. Moving with great care, he raised himself until he could look out: the chopper was a little below, and two or three hundred yards to the right, searching the forward slopes of the mountain.

Of course the pilot would know they had escaped the valley. MacConnachie expected that: he knew the pilot did not believe them dead. But he needed to see whether search parties were coming up, or whether it was still the pilot alone who held this conviction. He wriggled to the precipice and peered down.

There was plenty of activity. The fire was out, and across the stalk fields there spread a large brown stain, smoky with mist. But throughout the rest of the valley soldiers were milling about in abundance, conducting a hut-to-hut and thicket-to-thicket search. None of them had so far mounted the slopes below, so there was no immediate threat. But one thing was clear. The boy had talked. They were known to be alive.

With a sigh, he settled back and tried to make a proper military appreciation of their situation.

At the moment they held the high ground and the initiative. Above, slope mounted upon precipitous slope until the peak was lost from view. Below, the faces of rock were equally vertical; they could not be taken by surprise. And all over the face of the mountain were many thousands of jagged cuts and scars, in one of which they now lay. Even from the helicopter it would be impossible to spot them. A man three feet away could pass by unaware.

The Goons had failed to recapture them where they most needed to succeed, and now the odds lay with MacConnachie and Ansell. The pilot was the one remaining hope of encompassing their defeat, and he would know it. But there was one major flaw. And this, too, the pilot knew. And so, therefore, did the Goons.

They had to return to the valley. They had no choice. Without food they could never cross the mountains. And once up there in the high country, they would find nothing to help them: no animals, human or otherwise; no vegetation; nothing that lived. MacConnachie had always thought of it as the territory that Nature had forgotten, and it chilled him. Whatever they were to eat they must take with them, or in that alien environment they would die.

So for one whole day they had to linger in the lower slopes, and for one more night they must commit themselves to an order of battle that favoured the enemy. Having seized the initiative they would have, in effect, deliberately to relinquish it.

Fretting, MacConnachie kept watch, waiting for Ansell to wake. Perhaps Ansell would have some other suggestion.

As he sat there, MacConnachie began to understand how much he had been hurt during the preceding days. His arms, legs and torso ached without ease. Somewhere just out of reach, but close at hand, there stood a vast backlog of fatigue waiting to engulf him. He couldn't feel his left hand where the rope had cut in, where the piece of filthy cloth clung fast. But it was a trivial wound. He pinched it. He still couldn't feel it. The other hand, both hands, were dark with muck deeply ingrained; the tips of his fingers had lost their clarity of outline, being nailless, spongy, blood-stained extremities of flesh. The knees were scraped and dirty, protruding through the torn slacks he had put on at night. And the burns. His face felt stiff and unmoving as a mask. To produce an expression would be to crack the exterior carapace, and what would then come out?

He was not an imaginative man, but he was a man in pain. He held himself with the fixed formality of a wounded toy. The sleeping Ansell he did not even recognize. Tears came to his eyes, but he had no idea that he was weeping; and as they ran down his insensitive cheeks he felt nothing.

MacConnachie was a big man of immense physical stature and great natural beauty in his bodily proportions. Or rather, he had been. What he mourned now, unaware, was the first onset of ruin in a noble structure.

Ansell lay for some moments without opening his eyes. Although he didn't know it, he had slept for eight hours; MacConnachie had slept for three. Ansell was aware of a sense of enormous lassitude. Then he felt the sun burning him, and sat up with a start of remembrance. The pain leapt from his shoulder to wrap round his face like a red-hot cobweb; he gasped.

'Are you all right?'

'Yes.'

It was as though his entire body had been flayed with innumerable rods and then plunged into a vat of boiling water. He hung forward from the waist, recovering. MacConnachie remained silent. At last Ansell looked at the sun.

'It's late.'

'Midday.'

'Have you eaten?'

'No.'

'You didn't wait for me?'

'Why not?'

'You're a fool.'

Ansell knew that he sounded querulous, but he couldn't help himself. He said,

'Where are we?'

'Over the valley.'

'Is that the chopper?'

'Yes.'

'What are we going to eat?'

'Meat.'

'The last tin?'

'Yes, the last tin.'

With the minimum display of movement, MacConnachie removed the tin from the case, and started to attack its top with the knife. He said,

'This afternoon we select a hut or group of huts specifically, and a route in and out. Tonight, we attack.'

'We've no choice?'

'Not unless you can suggest one.'

The helicopter was drawing closer. MacConnachie seemed to be having greater difficulty than usual in opening the tin with blunted fingers. Ansell said,

'Are there no villages in the mountains?'

'There is nothing.'

'Could we attack the valley in an unexpected place?'

'There are no unexpected places. We've just so much time and energy left. We must use both where they'll count.'

The engine noise was loud now, the swish of blades clearly audible. Ansell said,

'If we go after water, the well will be right in the centre of the village.'

MacConnachie looked at him.

'That's right.'

The helicopter was upon them, and MacConnachie lay back, shielding the tin with his big hands. Ansell leaned under the rim of the depression. The chopper floated into view; it was an extraordinary sensation having it so close and even a little below him, as though he could reach out and touch it. The pilot and observer were clearly visible. It was evident that they had only a vague idea of where to search, and were conducting a series of quick, preliminary swoops, with the vain hope perhaps of catching them unawares. At one moment the machine came right up to the lip of their depression, peering, as it were, like a fly into an ashtray. Then it was gone, the sound deadened at once by an outcrop close at hand. Ansell said,

'The boy talked.'

'Yes.'

MacConnachie gouged out half the contents of the tin, which he had now managed to open, divided it into two equal portions and passed one to Ansell. The tin he returned to the suitcase, roping it against a sudden move. Then they ate breakfast, forcing the meat down, for they were neither of them hungry. Ansell said,

'Can't blame him. Probably had it beaten out of him. Parents are like that.'

'Were yours?'

'No. Were yours?'

'No.'

It was difficult to think of MacConnachie as a child. A thought suddenly came to Ansell. He indicated the helicopter with his head.

'How long's he been up there?'

'Since dawn.'

'Were you awake then?'

'Just after.'

'Get some sleep. I'll keep watch.'

MacConnachie accepted this without argument, saying,

'Wake me if they start coming up. And let me know what you think of the village.'

He was asleep at once. His implication was clear. He was leaving Ansell to plan the raid on the village.

It seemed to Ansell a long time since he had thought of the sun as their principal discomfort but now, and throughout the long oppression of the afternoon, it sat heavily upon him, compounding his pain. The sweat ran down and dried on his face; to wipe it off was a stinging agony. The brass bowl of the sky contained him.

Suddenly, towards evening, it grew quickly and unexpectedly dark. None of the Goon units had made any attempt to scale the lower slopes, which puzzled and disconcerted him. He woke MacConnachie while there was still light enough to test his suggestions against MacConnachie's instinct and experience.

MacConnachie noticed the sky at once.

'What time is it?'

'Not dusk, I'm sure.'

MacConnachie knew what it meant.

'The rains.'

'Oh God. When?'

'Within a week.'

He should have know the night before, the air had been full of it. Had he not been so tired and uncertain, he would have made the logical deduction. He said,

'Not to worry. Show me what you've decided.'

From this side of the valley, the village was now on their right. The river emerged from the delta at its heart to pass across their front and disappear to the left. Apart from one cursory glance at this left-hand end of the valley floor, they ignored it. Between them and the river system stood a narrow belt of fields and then the outgoing mud-flats, both of which they had traversed the night before, and which now constituted the terrain over which they would operate tonight. The pilot, having read the sky and knowing that further search before morning would prove fruitless, had flown out. Ansell said,

'There's a tree I want to identify to you.'

'I see it. Two o'clock; bushy-topped; right on the dividing line between the fields and the mud-flats.'

'That's the one. Stands out a mile. I'm sure we'll be able to see it from anywhere on the ground. We can use it as a base and a beacon.'

'Well done. Next?'

'Look at the village. Two main roads form an H.

'Yes.'

'The well is at the most distant crossroads, in the square.

'Christ, it's nearly out the other side.'

'Yes, we'll have to go through nearly the whole of the village to get there.'

'Why not round?'

'There are more Goons outside the village than in it. Once we penetrate the perimeter, we'll have a better chance on the back streets. I'm sure. I've been watching all afternoon.'

It was growing darker. Lights were coming on in the village, especially around the main streets. For some moments Mac-Connachie stared down, then he nodded in agreement.

'All right. What routes have you chosen?'

'Straight down to the bottom of the mountain. Then diagonally across the fields to the tree. We don't go on to the mudflats at all.'

MacConnachie shook his head decisively.

'No.'

'Why not?'

'Look at the Goons. First, they'll put a line of sentries all along the foot of this mountain. Second, they've already set up mobile patrols—see them?—in those fields.'

'So?'

'If we go for the tree diagonally, we'll be moving diagonally across their front; that way we treble the number of patrols we're likely to bump. No, we'll go straight to the mud-flats, then move along the edge of them to the tree; that way we'll be on the same line as the patrols and we'll see them coming. Never move diagonally across an enemy's front.'

They might have been in a lecture hut. Ansell said,

'Yes, Mac.'

'Have you picked specific target huts?'

'No. I've tried, but it doesn't work. They all seem to be inhabited. We'll have to choose when we're down there.'

'Fair enough. Do we go for water first, or food?'

Ansell was touched at the conscientious way in which MacConnachie consulted him on every decision. The blue shadows darkened, and he spoke more rapidly now:

'Food first.'

'Why?'

'The water is stale, but it'll last. And replenishing it involves the greatest risk. We can always abandon that part of the plan if we have to. Food we've got to have. We need as much time as possible to hit the huts.'

'Good. You've done well. We go in one up, one down, in fifteen minutes.'

Ansell started in surprise.

'So soon?'

'They'll expect us later. We just might catch them night-sloppy, before they're in position or properly adjusted.'

'But the whole place will still be awake.'

Dusk had swept up the mountain-side, and it was possible to stand without being seen. MacConnachie rose before he said, gently,

'Kid, they'll stay awake tonight, whatever happens.'

And then Ansell knew that his growing apprehensions had been confirmed. After a silence, he said quietly,

'Mac.'

'Yes?'

'Tell me why they haven't left the valley and come up after us.'

MacConnachie had untied the suitcase, and now settled to clean and oil the gun. He said,

'Kid, you know why.'

'Yes.'

'They're waiting for us. They know we're coming down again.'

'Yes.'

'They had a hut-to-hut this morning, but it wasn't a search. They want to be sure no hut is empty tonight. There'll be a farmer or a Goon in every one, armed and waiting.'

'We'll have to kill again.'

'Oh, yes.'

Ansell rose and stretched himself, setting fire to all the aches and pains now inherent in his body. It was a sharp reminder of how daunting the night would be. He said,

'There's nothing we can ditch?'

'No, we'd never find it again.'

'It's getting cold.'

'Do you want to eat?'

'No.'

'We'll eat before we sleep, then.'

Ansell had a pee. MacConnachie finished with the gun and changed its magazine for the fuller one they had wrested from the helicopter. Before tying up the case, he took out the razor and laid it to one side. Then, when all their equipment had been checked, he stropped the razor carefully against his boot.

'Cut-throat,' he said.

They left the depression and descended the forward slopes of the mountain. The night was very dark. Below, they could see a panorama of twinkling lights, richly studded to the right, then fading to a thin necklet of isolated glimmers at their left. It was not unlike looking down into the cavern of the sky. The ribbons of water were barely visible except where they bore a lamp's reflection diffused on the surface.

Forty feet above the level valley floor, MacConnachie signalled for stillness and crouched, waiting. One by one, he picked out the sentries stationed at fifteen-yard intervals along the foot of the mountain. In the field beyond, the dim shapes of patrols drifted past.

MacConnachie was looking for the idle man, the careless one who shifted too much, who coughed and became bored or frightened on sentry duty; there was always one. In two minutes he found him; or rather, the man advertised himself with a poorly suppressed trumpeting into his handkerchief. MacConnachie at once led the way to the right until they crouched directly above him.

For five minutes MacConnachie watched, without moving. It was unnaturally quiet; even the villagers were less talkative as though, in the distance, they had caught the whiff of blood. Dogs were restive, calling with solemn disquiet. The village was no more than half a mile to his right; the tree five hundred yards, almost to his front.

In that five minutes, three patrols passed in the field, giving him some idea of their density. On each occasion the idle sentry looked back over his shoulder as though to reassure himself that he had not been deserted. Such a man is always more concerned with his own discomfort than with his unit's purpose; at the next clear opportunity, MacConnachie led the way, slipping past him, breaking the cordon without trouble at its weakest link and leaving the man, oblivious of their passage, to his inefficiently performed duties.

The field was covered only with short stubble, but the darkness of the night and the natural dullness of the earth afforded some protection. As long as they did not find themselves lying directly in the path of a patrol that they had spotted too late, they should have a reasonable chance of traversing it. Inching snake-like over the soft, irrigated soil, MacConnachie led the way towards the mud-flats, the cool air heavy against their damaged cheeks.

Seventeen times they were forced to stop and lie in aching stillness on their journey to the flats. Once a patrol came so close that they poised themselves to strike; and at no time were they longer than a minute without the sight of one or another group of dim figures making their way through the shadows close at hand. But at last MacConnachie saw the gleam of the mud-flats ahead and, turning to the right, led the way towards the tall shape of the tree against the sky.

They started now to pass isolated huts, but MacConnachie considered it essential to establish a fixed base at the tree before they struck. In any case, he was puzzled: he couldn't understand why the huts were dark; the Goons should have ordered every lamp in the valley to be lit, it was the logical procedure. It could hardly be that the Goons hoped to lure them more deeply in; they had no choice but to come, and the Goons knew it. Because he did not understand, he fretted.

They were moving now along the same line as the patrols

and although, as he had predicted, those to their front were easier to spot, he had become concerned at the possibility that one might approach from the rear while they were halted. But they reached a point thirty yards from the tree without jeopardy, and flattened themselves to read the terrain ahead.

It was then that their situation deteriorated abruptly. MacConnachie had not sensed the danger but the moment Ansell, having seen it, gripped his arm, he too saw.

Around the base of the tree was spread out a brilliantly disguised ambush; probably there was a man up in the branches as well. He could see listening devices mounted on low tripods, and larger shapes which he took to be floodlights. So they had been out-thought. Some clever bastard, probably the pilot, had projected himself into their situation, had selected their route and found their fixed base. Perhaps they had already been pinpointed. Certainly fresh water was now denied them. He should have guessed this would happen. He must be more tired than he had thought.

Although a fixed base was not vital to their type of raid, thus to be denied it hurt MacConnachie, setting him at odds with the neatness of his operational method, and causing him to feel a nagging sense of imminent betrayal.

The shapes in ambush gave no indication that they had been detected. We don't deserve such luck, Ansell thought. I should have anticipated this. I'm supposed to be the brains.

Because he felt he had betrayed MacConnachie, Ansell strove frantically to reassess their position. They couldn't attack huts this side of the ambush; such huts would be empty shells, or the ambush was without point. They couldn't turn back and strike in the other end of the valley; time and enemy-strength denied it. They couldn't pull out altogether; without food they would be dead within a week. And there was no question now of raiding

163

the well; however great the force at the tree, a force of much greater size would be guarding the water supply.

They could only go round the ambush, and attack the huts behind it. They still held the initiative: they knew where the enemy were; the enemy did not yet know where they were. But, dear God, they would have to be quiet. They would have to steal and kill and slip away in desperate silence.

MacConnachie touched his arm and pointed with great caution out to the right in a slow sweeping movement. Mac had come to the same conclusion as himself: they must swing to the right, curving through the fields; the mud-flats would betray them in an instant.

As MacConnachie, flat against the earth, backed off carefully, Ansell looked behind him—and touched MacConnachie at once in warning.

MacConnachie looked behind him. A patrol was coming up the very path he had feared, rolling up their rear; unless they moved at once, they were in the direct line of contact. He turned to Ansell, but Ansell had anticipated him, beginning now to worm his way sideways to the right. MacConnachie followed.

Time was short and this was a manoeuvre that, with listening devices immediately ahead, demanded the most exquisite nervous and physical control. They could not hope to get far. But as the patrol came closer it served to help as well as to threaten them, for its own noises, however slight, would confuse the electronic ears, masking any sound that they themselves might make. Ansell seemed to understand this; he increased the rate of progress very slightly until, with the patrol very near, they were compelled to stop for fear of being seen. They could then only bury their faces and wait.

The swish of feet through stubble, the grunt of laboured breathing, drew closer, and passed; and as the last man padded out of earshot, they looked up cautiously. The Goons' discipline was excellent: the patrol approached and walked through the ambush without the smallest indication that it was there, disappearing into the shadows beyond.

The swing out to the right was a slow, painful and laborious business, with Ansell of necessity in the lead. It wasn't the patrols, to which they had grown accustomed and which they could easily slip, that oppressed them, but the awareness of those unnaturally powerful ears reaching out above their heads from the left. Until they had passed a point level with the tree they had to concern themselves primarily with the listening devices. After that, no soldier would point such a machine towards the village since the normal night-sounds of the population, however hushed, would render it useless.

At last they were clear and they rested a moment, easing the painful tension out of their limbs and looking ahead. The lights of the village were now very close, the outskirts no more than three hundred yards away. Ansell knew that MacConnachie was waiting for him to give a lead, but try as he might he could not make the image of what he saw now knit with the image he had seen that afternoon. There were perhaps a dozen isolated huts spread out between themselves and the village, but at this level, and with the lights beyond, it was impossible to judge distances. He would simply have to pick one at random, and then they would have to recce it before striking.

Down to the left, close to the edge of the mud-flats, stood one hut quite alone, a dim glow of light showing beyond its farthest corners. The door must face towards the river. He indicated it to MacConnachie.

MacConnachie looked at it, then looked towards the tree. Ansell knew what he was thinking: to reach it they must pass between the ambush and the village. But Ansell was convinced that subconsciously the Goons would believe them unable to bypass the listening post; and even a few minutes' observation had demonstrated that, knowing it was there, the patrols were disinclined to search behind it and were concentrating on the fields and the mud-flats. In essence, their situation was a simple one: so long as they remained unlocated, they remained in command of the situation; but on the instant of their detection, all the disconnected eyes and ears now searching and probing for them would become one, bent on their recapture, and the initiative would pass decisively into enemy hands. Wherever they walked in the valley, they walked with death; they might as well accept it now.

It seemed that MacConnachie did. He checked to make sure that Ansell had the knife at the ready and passed the suitcase back to him. Then, in the pale wash of light from the village, Ansell saw MacConnachie draw the razor from his boot, open it, and clutch it in his right hand.

Their war narrowed down to the hut that stood alone, the village on their right, the ambush on their left, and the ground in between. Ansell's face burned. The night air was stiflingly heavy, the earth cold against his stomach. Slowly, slowly they inched forward, pausing, watching, waiting, listening, crawling forward again. The hut came to meet them with agonizing slowness, yet Ansell found that he was not afraid. It may have been the sense of having a defined objective that encouraged him.

They saw only one patrol, but it was a vital one. It came from the left, passing through the ambush and moving past the hut on its farther side, before it was lost from view in the shadows to their right; it warned them that the hut stood on a regular patrol route along the edge of the mud-flats and that they would have to wait for the next visit, timing it.

MacConnachie decided that, once the next patrol had passed through, they would approach the hut from the right. They had to see the front before they attacked it, and from that side they would get the maximum warning if the third patrol came early.

They sweated and waited. At last the patrol came and went. The interval was ten minutes. That was the extent of time they had to reconnoitre and, during the next gap, to strike.

He led the way to an observation point. He estimated that they had been in the valley two and a half hours.

There was a Goon on guard in front of the door. Again, MacConnachie marvelled at the discipline of such men, that they could pass at night without speaking. They must want us very badly, he thought. He waited until Ansell had thoroughly absorbed their predicament, then led the way back to their former position, from which they could no longer see the sentry; they couldn't afford to linger on the patrol route.

For some moments he thought, then he put his lips to Ansell's ear:

'I want you to kill the sentry. Go under the hut. Immediately the next patrol has passed.'

He waited for Ansell's nod, then took the fish knife and gave Ansell the razor.

It had been a difficult decision for MacConnachie to make. But Ansell was the better stalker, and now this gift must be put to use. He was also a trained killer. He knew how it should be done; he must learn that it *could* be done, and that he could do it.

In truth, MacConnachie had discovered that his senses were deserting him. He could no longer see as clearly as once he did, and his ears felt curiously muffled. The gift might be as sharp as ever, but the eyes failed, and the clarity of hearing was gone; it had been Ansell who had seen the ambush first.

All evening, he now realized, he had operated by 'feel'; but it was not until this moment that he understood how much he had come to depend on the gift. He could no longer trust himself to make this kill, for the gift would not help him: it was a matter of poise, observation, timing; all the senses tuned to an exact pitch. He must be very tired.

He had to rely on Ansell. This was something he had never done before. Or had he? Had he known, and prepared for this moment, during the afternoon?

That had been a bad time, in the water, when the gift had left him.

Or *had* it been when he was in the water?

He could not remember.

Ansell held the razor in his hand.

Kill the sentry. He had killed before. He had killed the farmer. He had kicked until the teeth shattered and split from the gums, and the jaw went awry, and the blood came out as foam. The man had gone on screaming. The sentry must die quietly. Quick, clean, without fuss.

The blade towards you, at a slight angle. One hand over the mouth. We don't want him shouting, do we? Tilt the head back. Remember to bring your hand up close to the neck so he can't get his arm inside it. Then one neat swift movement, across, in that manner there. If you have to cut again, cut quickly. And don't forget, blood makes a noise on a hard surface. So lean him forward. If you're on a flat, hard surface, always lean him forward. And keep your hand clamped over his mouth for at least ten seconds. He'll go on living that long. Even if you have his head right off, he'll still live for six seconds. And *lay* him down, like a baby, don't drop him. And never waste time hiding him, you can't hide the blood. Right, next!

There was a gap just under the hut, between the bottom of the hut and the soil. Perhaps the river floods sometimes. There'll be two steps and a pair of feet. If you can't see the feet, go for the steps. You'll have to come out in one swift movement. If he sees you coming it doesn't matter, so long as he makes no sound.

Crawl halfway, then rise; the hut will mask the rest of your approach.

I wonder what were the last words he heard on earth? He has already heard them.

The patrol came and went. No one spoke to the sentry. MacConnachie touched Ansell, and Ansell crawled away towards the hut. MacConnachie thought: we've got ten minutes at most. The moment the next patrol sees the body, or sees that the sentry is missing, secrecy will be gone. We must be into that hut like a streak. There's a light inside, it's bound to show. How much does it matter? Have orders been given not to open any door without first dimming the lamp? And why the hell is the valley so dark? I wish I could work out the answer to that one.

He rubbed the scar in the canteen which Ansell had left at his side, worrying.

At the side of the hut Ansell dropped to his knees, feeling underneath to see what sort of surface he would have to crawl over. It was cool, damp earth; ideal.

He flattened himself and inched forward until he was completely under the hut. The air had a stale liquidity that was unexpectedly refreshing. In front of him was a low, long strip of visible landscape bordered at the top by the floor of the building. No steps. Two feet, and the bottom half of two legs forming the traditional shape of a soldier in battle dress.

He readjusted the razor to its correct position and crawled forward until, within a few minutes, he lay immediately behind the booted feet which were only twelve inches from his face. He breathed deeply, quietly, half a dozen times. Then, as he inched forward a fraction at a time, the base of the hut fell back until, eyes angled upwards, he could look up the entire length of his adversary's body. From this position the great trunks of the legs led to a small body and a smaller head. The man was looking to his left but now he turned to look to the right. Ansell remained absolutely still. He could see nothing of the man's features. The light from under the door drew a wobbly line across from the back of one trouser-leg to the back of the other. The man looked to his front.

Ansell drew carefully back. He was right handed; the man was in perfect position. He took another slow, deep breath, poising himself: He worked his right leg cautiously up the side of his prone body, bending the knee, flattening the foot against the earth; from that leg would come the motive power for his spring. He felt the razor to be correctly gripped. He inched his left hand forward, leaning into the soil until he reached the point of true balance. He took one more slow breath.

He came forward, up and out in one swift movement. His left hand clamped over the mouth, his right punched forward, the razor bit deeply in and the blood spouted startlingly as he drew his hand across. He was aware that he carved too severely. The man raised no noticeable physical objection. Ansell kept his left arm rigidly locked, finding that he could pinch the nostrils now as well, pulling the head back against his own mouth, breathing through the musty locks of the other man's hair. His helmet must have fallen off.

As the knees sagged Ansell bent forward with him, holding him close, gripping tightly to the head, feeling the warmth of the other body against his own. There was a hot, radishy smell in the air, primitively exciting. As the body slumped farther, putting its full weight on Ansell's arms, the head tilted back, alone supporting the torso from dropping to earth. There was a striking freedom of play in this head as though at any moment it might come free entirely, to be left, as a trophy, in Ansell's embrace.

MacConnachie loomed up beside him.

'Put him down!'

As Ansell broke off his dance with the corpse and let it fall, MacConnachie stooped and picked up the sentry's gun, thrusting it at Ansell. With barely any hesitation he opened the door, dropped low and dived through it. A glance told him that the room was unoccupied. He went at once to the lamp and stood in front of it, masking it, until Ansell had come in after him, when he hissed urgently, 'Shut the door!'

Ansell shut it. There was blood on his hands.

MacConnachie had not realized how empty the hut was until he looked now, carefully, all round it. There was a table, a chair, a pallet bed without coverings; nothing more. Nothing else at all. Bare walls; bare floor. The hut had been stripped of anything that could be carried and might be useful to them. The lamp burning in the centre of the table was, apart from themselves, the only object to display any appearance of animation.

Ansell made a noise. MacConnachie turned. Ansell was staring at him, eyes forced wide open in shocked realization.

'There's nothing here!'

'Shh!'

'There's nothing here!'

It was as though, in a whisper, in something less than a whisper, Ansell was screaming at the top of his voice. He had blood on his chin.

MacConnachie turned out the lamp.

'Come on!'

He went through the door without looking to see if Ansell followed. Caution was no more than a reflex now. The one thing that could save them would be outrageous boldness and resolution.

He went straight to the canteen and suitcase which he had left outside, turned to hang the canteen on Ansell, then set out at a fast open walk towards the next hut, farther along the edge of the mud-flats but closer to the village. In forty seconds he was there, closing rapidly on the sentry who stood at the door. He let the case fall, dropped the gun, and went in with the fish knife. The sentry saw him coming. He turned towards him, bringing up his gun, but his whole manner was redolent of a profound and inhibiting uncertainty, so undisguised was MacConnachie's approach. MacConnachie walked straight up to him and killed him with the knife and the boot, one small cry of surprise alone escaping.

As Ansell came up laden with two guns, the razor, suitcase and canteen, MacConnachie whispered, 'Wait here!'

He was into and out of the second hut in thirty seconds. It was as naked as the first; they had been again out-thought, and were now alone and helpless.

A shout rose up from the far side of the nearest water. Mac-Connachie bent, took up the dead sentry's helmet and clamped it on to Ansell's head, pulling the strap roughly down under his chin.

'Wait here!' he said again, and ran back towards the first hut, vanishing in shadow.

The shout came again. A shot was fired. Ansell saw the flash from across the water, but heard no bullet fall. In a dazed condition he knelt and searched the sentry's body for magazines, which he stuffed into his frayed jacket pockets. Then a burst of firing came from across the river and bullets smacked into the front of the hut at his side. MacConnachie came running back. He, too, now had a steel helmet on his head.

'Come on!'

They ran at a crouch towards the mountains, passing across the front of the village lights and presenting themselves in silhouette to the men in ambush. Speed was of the essence: for a few moments there would be confusion as figures ran towards the sound of shooting; no one would have a clear idea of where they were or who was firing. They both knew too well the vital nature of the coming seconds.

Whistles were blowing and the firing had stopped. There came a dull, flat whoosh of sound and a few seconds later a red star shell exploded in the sky. A mortar had been fired from the ambush position. At this signal, lights appeared all over the valley. It was clear what had happened: the sentries had opened the doors of the huts they were guarding and brought the lamps out into the open, turning them up to their fullest extent; MacConnachie now had the answer to his question.

All of this came to him precipitately in the sharpened awareness of flight.

Now, at three points, great swathes of light lit up the stubble in the fields as previously sited floodlights were brought into play. Those at the ambush point were angled away from them; glancing hurriedly in that direction, MacConnachie saw a finger of light wave raggedly at the sky and knew that the lights were being turned towards the village and towards them. The other areas of bright light were too distant to be a danger.

His sole concern was to close the gap between themselves and the foot of the mountain as rapidly as possible, and this they were doing by running flat out. There was still a great deal of confusion; patrols ran past quite close, all of them towards the scene of the shooting, and all dully tinged with scarlet by the parachute flare suspended in the sky. The whistles took up a different chant, issuing instructions and passing information. There was no more shooting yet. It didn't matter where they hit the rock wall, they would start climbing at once. The perimeter guard would still be intact along the foot of the heights. Even the idle man should be alert by now.

A hundred and fifty yards to go. A figure rose up in MacConnachie's path; he smashed him down with the butt of his gun. Now isolated shots were fired from the direction of the ambush, but MacConnachie could hear no sound of bullets' passage through the air.

A hundred yards, and there was shouting again. Far away to the right a lone gun fired a burst. And now what MacConnachie had been waiting for and hoping to beat occurred: the mortar started to fire again to the logical pre-set pattern. Star shell. There was a slight pause after the whoosh of discharge, and then the whole scene was lit with a sudden, garish light. It was all a matter of luck now. While he and Ansell had only to reach the mountain, the Goons would have to locate, aim and fire with their night eyes half blinded by the dazzling purity of the flare's brightness.

He drove himself to accelerate, watching the rise and fall of the ground beneath his feet to give his eyes a moment to adjust from night vision, before he looked up to seek out the perimeter guards. Fortunately he and Ansell were coming out of the light towards them, and that would help.

Now the guns started to fire controlled bursts behind them, and the pitch of the whistles changed. They screamed, Contact, Contact! The whisper of bullets came to him, but the range was long and the burp gun is a close-quarter weapon. The mortar was pumping star shell into the sky as fast as it could fire. The sentries at the perimeter were sharply alert, looking this way and that with weapons raised, but it was clear they had not yet spotted the rushing shapes of MacConnachie and Ansell.

Thirty yards to go. Bullets slapped into the earth all around them, half-spent and less than dangerous. But now one of the perimeter guards spotted them and started to fire. MacConnachie broke right, away from the man, and picking one particular sentry ran straight at him, roaring at the top of his voice. The firing man was having to change position constantly to maintain a clear field of view, taking hurried aim, firing, then running forward a little before he could take aim again; he was ineffective.

But he had activated his comrades; they, too, had now seen the roaring figures—for Ansell had taken up MacConnachie's battle cry—and were attempting, like the first man, to close the gap and fire accurately at the same time.

The man directly in MacConnachie's path had panicked. He was edging to his right, firing from the hip and forgetting to aim low; the bullets passed harmlessly above MacConnachie's head.

They were now very close, not twenty feet to cover. The Goons were trying in messy, disorganized formation to press in from left and right. MacConnachie heard Ansell fire, and one man tumbled down to his right: fluke shot; running, and without proper aim, a discharge might be expected to take psychological rather than effective toll of an enemy.

In their anxiety to stop them, the Goons to their rear were getting careless and firing many shots into the wavering rank of their own men. Another man went down, clutching at his thigh; neither MacConnachie nor Ansell had fired at that moment. It was evident that the mountain guard had been disconcerted by the suddenness of the charge, the pitch of Ansell and MacConnachie's redoubtable screaming, and the daunting realization that they were being fired on by their own side. Confusion grew among them.

Then MacConnachie and Ansell were into the line and MacConnachie fired one-handed from the hip, clutching the suitcase in his other hand. The nearest man flew back, mouth agape, arms flung wide, his weapon spinning off into the shadows. MacConnachie passed through the line, dropped the case, turned left, and got off four shots at close range, aiming as carefully as his trembling arms and heaving chest would allow. Two shots took effect. He could hear Ansell, at his back, firing single-shot, and knew that he had seen his own manoeuvre and imitated it, shooting into the right flank of the line.

The moment he was sure the guards had been cowed and

the fire fight temporarily won, he shouted over his shoulder, 'Piss off!'

He saw Ansell scramble up the slope, pulling the suitcase after him. He fired once more into the left flank, then turned to engage the right, now left in the air by Ansell's departure. In doing so, he caught a glimpse of the situation in the valley. Many hundreds of the enemy were pressing in from all sides, shooting as they came; they were far closer than he had expected.

Now one of the guard came charging at him and he was compelled to drop to his knees, take careful aim and fire three times before the man stopped coming. It was like killing one of his own, so determinedly was the assault pressed home.

Bullets sang off the rocks on every quarter, above and beside him. He was at an impossible disadvantage in that he couldn't fire a burst, he had to conserve ammunition for the remainder of their journey, so much more potentially dangerous now that they lacked supplies. He knew there was nothing remarkable in his remaining so far unhit—the Goons, too, had to fire from the hip while running—but the superior numbers of shots discharged must take effect at any moment. He waited for Ansell to open covering fire above. It was past time to pull out.

Then he heard Ansell's gun fire in well-judged single-shot, and saw first one man and then another spin out of the line to his front. The range was only thirty yards. He turned and scrabbled furiously up the face of the mountain.

The Goons were brilliantly lit by their own flares and in the natural killing-ground from Ansell's point of view—fifty feet, directly below—he could hardly fail to take out an enemy with every shot. But he didn't want to waste ammunition, so he contented himself with striking only at those men who, from their stance, were clearly following the passage of MacConnachie's flight and actually aiming at him.

Then MacConnachie was beside him, gasping, 'Let's go!'

They went up the mountain, Ansell hanging back this time to cover the rear, MacConnachie once more in the lead with the suitcase.

It was a matter now of disengaging from the enemy, and here the factors all favoured them: they held the high ground, dominating an enemy who was forced to climb no faster than they did, and always under the threat of their guns; they were traversing a terrain riven confusingly with opportunities for an unseen change of direction, and never more than half revealed by even the closest flare. When the mortar man moved closer to the mountain, the illumination he provided was more useful to them than to their enemies since, while it outlined the Goons as perfect targets, it did nothing to improve the Goons' visibility of them.

Someone threw a grenade, but this method was abandoned at once to a howl of execration. To throw grenades uphill is a doubtful procedure at any time; to do it by night on a hillside crowded with your own men is to invite disaster.

MacConnachie and Ansell had simply to maintain a steady rate of progress, which they did. Only three times did they fire, on each occasion killing one man, to maintain their ascendancy over their pursuers. In a short while the star shell was discontinued and silence fell. Someone down below had got a grip on his men and brought them under proper control. Within an hour they had lost the Goons, and contact was once again successfully broken off.

MacConnachie kept going. He knew that the Goons would climb through the night, and that they would have to do the same. When morning came, the Goons would form up a defensive perimeter, and send patrols forward. They were in no hurry; they had overwhelming superiority of manpower, a secure supply-line, and eyes in the sky.

As the gap opened out, he began to think again of the helicopter as the greater threat and the infantry as the lesser. Of the raid on the valley he would not allow himself to think at all.

Ansell could not help thinking about it. He was desperately tired. He knew that he was using the last of his strength. His face ached without cease, and it seemed to him that what was left of his arms and legs operated without conscious instruction from him, propelling him endlessly to no particular destination—although he was never in fact more than two yards below MacConnachie all night.

The strangest phenomenon, though it was in no way alarming, was that his brain had deserted his cranium and was floating up the mountain-side before him. Far from being a hindrance, this proved to be a help, since he tried constantly, and with good humour, to rejoin it. All the time this brain worked busily, very light and clear, but with areas of mist and impenetrability.

The attack on the valley was a complete disaster. For the first time we brought death and took nothing. Not so. We took one gun and two magazines. Three, with the one already on the gun. We've got half a tin of meat left, and two of soup. I think it's two. My brain thinks it's two, too. And lost a knife. At least, I haven't got it, and I started out with it.

There was something else that Ansell and his brain could not quite reach. But to turn to other matters ...

We can no longer escape. We have no food, and no prospect of food. Without food, we cannot cross the mountains. Therefore we shall die. That's a clue. But to turn to other matters ...

Every hut was guarded, and every hut was empty. We gave no thought to this, as we gave no thought to the possibility of ambush. We must be very tired. Our brains must be very tired. The truth is, from the very beginning, we had *no chance at all* of making a successful raid on the valley. We should have known that. That's another clue.

178

You see, Mac, it's very simple. So simple that you can't see it. Message: *There are more of them than there are of us.* Message ends.

We have—now—no chance whatever.

But to turn to other ...

It was the killing of the sentry. Not the killing so close, with the man you are killing so tight in your arms as though you were loving him. But ... clue, too ... food, two, soup, two, too.

But to turn ...

It's to do with ... empty huts ... no chance.

It's ...

One of the necessary conditions—in morality—of a 'just war' —is that you should have—a—reasonable—prospect—of—success.

But we have none.

None.

This is nonsense.

Is there a point at which all the virtues Mac has—that I am learning so fast—that I aspire to—become vices? When killing is simply killing? Plain murder? Because we are directing our violence to no achievable end?

Oh, this is nonsense. What are we to do? Give ourselves up? Acknowledge defeat from within?

We raided the valley, and we came away with nothing. We were out-thought at every turn. We are hungry, we are cold. We are tired, and hurt, and without supplies or hope of any kind. Why should we worry?—Ansell smiled—we are already dead.

What a trick!

An hour before dawn, MacConnachie floundered to a stop. He turned to Ansell with the fraught petulance of a child who has been deceived.

'We must sleep. We *must!*'

He fell down. Ansell bent carefully, restraining the natural buoyancy of his body, to prevent that inflated bladder of flesh from taking off, and stroked MacConnachie's head. But he was already asleep, the helmet beside him like a spare skull.

What do you expect for ten cents a day and a bowl of rice? asked Ansell's brain. Hercules?

Oh, do be quiet, I want to sleep.

The seventh day, when God rested. Ansell had hardly slept at all when the sound of the helicopter's engine woke him. He forced his eyelids apart; they had stuck together at some point during the last hour. Then, realizing that he still sat upright, he lay carefully back. The helicopter flew over and disappeared above; he was still waiting for the sound to fade, when a quite unexpected modulation of pitch came back to him: the chopper was landing.

He frowned—or rather, he sent a message to his face that said 'frown', but nothing occurred; he was aware simply of resistance from his features, as though his facial skin had been encased in some sort of cocoon. This phenomenon he found faintly entertaining. He was tempted to essay the full range of expressions. He felt relaxed, lackadaisical, a little dizzy.

The helicopter flew out again, heading once more down into the valley. He supposed he ought to have a look to see if the Goons were coming up. He crawled to the nearest lip and peered over. Below him, small groups of infantry were working their way up the face of the mountain. The sun was hidden behind layers of grey, puffy cloud, but the air burned and the atmosphere was stifling. He went back to wake MacConnachie.

'The chopper flew over just now, landed, and flew out again.'
'Landed?'

'Yes.'

'That wasn't for a pee.'

'No. The Goons are above us. They're coming up from below too.'

For some moments MacConnachie lay very still, looking up at the sky. Then he slowly sat up as though he had wearied of the whole business and become bored by it. He said,

'I suppose we ought to move.'

'Yes.'

'It'll rain soon.'

'That'll make it harder for them.'

'And for us.'

MacConnachie opened the suitcase and brought out their last half-tin of meat. He sat staring dully down into the interior, pushing their few remaining possessions this way and that as though he had forgotten what he was doing. Then he pulled the fish knife from under his body. So that's where it was, thought Ansell. MacConnachie scooped out his share, then passed the tin to Ansell, eating his own from the end of the blade. Ansell found the meat quite without taste of any kind but, although he was in no way hungry, he swallowed it down. The helicopter flew over again, landed, and departed. Neither man paid any attention to this intrusion upon a private picnic. He looks something less than human, thought Ansell, watching the darker hole open in MacConnachie's filthy, stiff, crystalline mask, and the gobbets of substance disappear within; I must look the same. The mask said,

'There must be a shelf of some kind up there.'

They drank, putting the stale hole of the canteen to the stale holes of their mouths. It transpired that when MacConnachie ran back to the sentry Ansell had killed, he stole not only the steel helmet but the two spare magazines as well. When he learned that Ansell had done the same at the second hut, he seemed for a moment to gain a new lease of life. His gun still held six rounds, Ansell's eight, and there were eight left in the magazine he had replaced before the valley raid. By putting all of this ammunition into one magazine, they were left with four full magazines, a further magazine with twenty-two rounds in it, and two empty ones.

He put the twenty-two-round magazine on to his own gun, telling Ansell to put a full magazine on his. They then had three full magazines in reserve: one hundred and twenty-two bullets in all.

Since the terrain now abounded in safe hiding-places, he decided also to dispose of all the refuse they had collected on their journey. He therefore took the accumulation of empty tins from the case and stuffed them one by one deep into a fissure in the rock wall, thrusting the two empty magazines after them. He then repacked the case and roped it up, packing also the fish knife and the razor. For immediate action they were both armed; should they require the knives, they would have time to get at them.

Their order of march now involved the carrying of one gun to each man, two spare magazines by MacConnachie and one by Ansell, a steel helmet apiece, and the suitcase and canteen as before. Without noticing the fact, they had discontinued their routine of changing clothes at dusk and dawn. They now wore their jackets and slacks under the native coats at all times.

MacConnachie seemed to have relapsed into his previous indifference. The helicopter came and went with its third load, and MacConnachie watched it, staring into the sky long after it had gone. Two days ago, he would never have revealed his face to a searching chopper. Finally he turned to Ansell with pale eyes.

'There's not much point in going on, is there?'

'No.'

After a silence, Ansell added,

'But I suppose we will.'

'We might as well.'

The failure of the raid on the valley was not referred to. Those who are not here must make the moral decisions, Ansell thought; those who are, are too busy. But within himself he was aware that an important barrier had been crossed, and that a watershed of great significance now lay behind them.

As he climbed, MacConnachie leaned into the face of the mountain, straining to make headway against the steep slope of the rock wall and tearing his neck in the attempt to spot the shelf on which the Goons were located; but he couldn't see it. Both he and Ansell had slung their guns round their necks, with the weapons nestling uncomfortably in the small of the back and the straps tight about their throats. He would *have* to do something about the suitcase. He could no longer climb one-handed over this sort of stuff; he was too tired. There was, in any case, a great lassitude over him. Every action that the ascent demanded, he performed with the minimum of effort; he knew he must find some way to conserve a strength in which he was, quite suddenly, frighteningly deficient. It was almost as though Ansell had more in reserve than he had.

In a day, or two at the most, the rains would come and the Goons would bog down. So long as he and Ansell maintained progress, they could forget about the force to their rear. For the first four days of rain, perhaps for as long as a week, flying would be impossible and the Goons would lose their eyes as well. But the pilot was a man to take risks, and as the importance of his role grew, the danger inherent in the risks he would be willing to take would increase. Curtailed or not, he would be in the air at every opportunity, ignoring the threat of sudden, unpredictable downpours that could swamp him. So long as they ran, he would hunt; so long as they gambled their lives, he would gamble his; they were now his meat.

Somehow, despite the severity of the coming rains, he and Ansell must make full use of the week's grace they would provide.

He refused to think of their dwindling supplies, or to ask himself what would happen when the soup and paste ran out.

But one thought haunted him: the Goons had used the huts to lure them into an ambush in the valley; was he now right to fear that the ambush itself had been the bait for a larger trap, the jaws of which waited with the force on the shelf above?

And to the tail of this thought there was tied another: the water in the canteen would keep them alive for ten days, though after three they would cease to exist as a fighting unit. So had it really been such a blessing? Were they lucky, or were they cursed? The earth could curse a man. Nature could turn her face away.

But what had he done to offend Nature?

They had passed the shelf before he saw it. Then the helicopter came, and they watched it land and reinforce the party below. This time it remained in the vicinity, once more setting up its systematic pattern of search.

The sky was still heavy and fluffy, the sun hidden behind banked clouds, but the rays came through to burn them as they climbed on and the air, seeming grey, was stolidly oppressive.

Again and again MacConnachie tried to call up from his stomach that sense of unyielding purpose, but could never re-capture it for more than a moment or two. He could not become angry. The mountain towered above them, growing ever steeper as they rose above the ambush they had so fortuitously avoided. He could not see the peak. It would, in any case, only be the first of many. Already the rock face had taken on the scarred and barren look of high country, where nothing grows and no animal lives for long. All around them were endless pits and crags, horny scales of rock, angles and edges that slashed at the leather of their boots and skinned their legs. Their tattered slacks were now reduced to shreds, and the lower edges of their native coats were nibbled ragged by the jutting shards of stone.

In their stunned and ruined condition, progress was minimal. Apart from the danger of falling, MacConnachie knew they did too little to hide themselves. But simply to keep moving upwards was all his body or mind could encompass.

Ansell wallowed in a stupor, half asleep. His eyes went in and out of focus all the time, and he remained dizzy, grinding his way agonizingly upward. His brain had returned to his skull and burned there. Every time MacConnachie stopped, he stopped, sagging forward from the waist and sending his brain skidding down to the crown of his head, where it piled with a crash against the cranium wall. When MacConnachie started, he started, reversing the process and tilting his brain back between his ears with a soft, sickening swish.

Yet, despite this, he remained in some uncalculated way in touch with his surroundings. He knew, as from a great distance, that his body and one other were going through the motions of a ritual that had been built in: a drill that would keep them safe long after the driver had taken his hands from the controls of the mechanism.

Sort of a dead man's handle.

MacConnachie thought: there comes a moment when a man has to acknowledge that he is growing old. That he has grown old.

Then he waits for death.

No. He goes to meet it.

And he kicks its teeth in.

For three more hours, with little prompting from them, their arms and legs kept going. Then they stopped.

'This is stupid.'

'Yes.'

Silence.

Ansell said,

'I can see the bones of my finger-tips.'

'Look the other way.'

There was no sound from the helicopter now, and the sky grew darker.

'Tastes salty.'

Silence.

'Talk.'

'What about?'

'You're the brainy one.'

Silence.

'A man called Bertillon once worked out a method of identifying criminals.'

'What did he do?'

'Measured them.'

'Measured what?'

'Arms, legs, that sort of thing.'

'Tools?'

'I shouldn't think so.'

Silence.

'What about women?'

'Measured them, too.'

'What did he use?'

'Tape measure, I suppose.'

'Up and down, or across?'

'Probably judged by the size of their mouths.'

A dry, creaking sound came from MacConnachie. Ansell said, 'Is that true?'

'What?'

'You can tell by the size of their mouths?'

'Shouldn't think so. Never compared 'em.'

'There's something about wide lips though, isn't there?'

'There's something about Chinese women. That isn't true.'

'No, I never thought it was.'

'Don't you know?'

'No.'

'Never had one?'

'No.'

'You haven't missed anything.'

Silence.

'I've never had any woman.'

It took a moment or two for the full import of this to sink in. Then, tortured though he was by the wrenching of flesh involved, MacConnachie simply had to turn his head.

'What?'

'I've never slept with a woman in my life.'

Silence.

'You're joking!'

'No.'

MacConnachie had to pin it down, if only for the sake of his sanity:

'You've never had a bit?'

'No.'

'You've never laid a woman?'

'No.'

Silence.

'*Never?*'

'Never.'

Silence.

'Bloody hell.'

'Quite.'

MacConnachie was visited by a terrible sense of guilt and responsibility.

'What have I done to you?'

'It's nothing to do with you.'

'Kid, this is serious.'

'It's not that bad.'

'It's ... *terrifying*.'

MacConnachie was in a, to him, unaccustomed state of awe. Ansell said,

'There's not much we can do about it now, anyway.'

Then, as though to explain this incapacity, he added,

'I'm not—too beautiful—just at the moment.'

MacConnachie shook his head in wonderment and pain. He said urgently,

'First thing! When we get back—first thing!'

'We'll not get back, Mac. I've had it as far as the women are concerned. If I'd known. But you don't, do you?'

'Oh God. Christ.'

Silence.

'What's it like?'

'What?'

'Having a woman.'

'It's all right.'

'What do you do?'

'You shove it in, what do you think?'

'But what do you say?'

'What do you say? You just shove it in, that's all.'

'But there must be some lead-in ... '

'Well, of course there is! I don't know. You shove the bloody thing in, that's all. What do you want, for God's sake?'

'Tell me, Mac. You must have had lots of women.'

'Yeah, well ... that's different.'

'Why?'

'Different sort of woman.'

'From what?'

'The sort of woman you'd have.'

'What sort of woman would I have?'

MacConnachie controlled his exasperation.

'You tell me.'

Silence.

'Blonde. I've always hoped she'd be blonde. And small. With long, straight hair. And a tough, skinny body. And sexy.'

'Sounds okay.'

'But with terrific dignity, you know? So that she never seems sexy with other people, but when she's with me...'

'Sure, yeah.'

'Only what do you say to such a woman? How do you go about it?'

'She'd find a way.'

'But how can you tell when a woman's feeling sexy?'

'Well, it shows. In her face, and her... What do you want, for Christ's sake, a bloody lecture?'

'I suppose I do, yes.'

'Look, you can't... I mean, you don't just talk about that sort of thing. It... happens.'

'But what happens, Mac?'

'Sweet God Almighty...'

'I mean, the last time you had a woman, what did you do?'

'I tell you, it's not the same! It's a different sort of woman.'

'Why?'

'Your sort, you have to treat with style. The dinner, and... You can't just poke a woman like that.'

'Why not?'

'You should respect her! She's got... You don't just rush at her.'

'But don't you poke her just the same, whether you respect her or not?'

MacConnachie was outraged.

'Of course you don't! Christ, what do you think? This is no two-dollar lay you're talking about! You respect a woman like that. You treat her with... Now, you remember that, kid.'

'Yes, Mac.'

'You remember that.'

'Yes, Mac.'

Silence.

MacConnachie scowled.

'What do I know about it, anyway? I've never been near tail like that in my life. Every bit I've ever had, I've paid for. Well, that's right. That's fair. You don't want a woman cluttering up your life. Pox everything up for yourself.'

'No, Mac.'

'No, well—that's all right, then.'

Silence.

'But the—*mechanics* are the same, aren't they? Whether you pay or not? I mean, that's what I'd like to know about. I'd like to have done it just once, and not have to imagine. Nothing's ever the way you imagine it.'

MacConnachie felt a burning sense of grief, such as he had never experienced before on behalf of another human being. Awkwardly, he murmured,

'I'm sorry. I'm sorry, kid. I'm really sorry.'

'So am I.'

With painful seriousness, MacConnachie said,

'If I could find a woman. The right sort for you. I'd ...'

'I know. I know you would.'

MacConnachie shrugged.

'I'm sorry. We've had that.'

A silence.

'Do they enjoy it?'

'Why, sure. They love it, kid,' said MacConnachie, who had never seen anything but professional indifference in a woman's eyes in his life. 'They do everything they can to make it easy for you, and good. For themselves too.'

'I'm glad about that. They must, really, but you're never sure.'

' 'Course they do.'

'There was a chap called Tiresias. In Greek Mythology. He was supposed to have had it both ways. He said the women have the best of it, but I shouldn't have thought so.'

'No, that's a load of cobblers. You both have the best of it. That's the way it is.'

'I'm glad. That makes it good.'

'That's right. Sure.'

A silence.

'The right woman for me would have to be hairless and done to a turn. There can't be many of them about.'

'No, there must be pretty much of a shortage in that department.'

Silence.

'Are you cold, Mac?'

'Yes.'

'So am I.'

'We'll move again in a minute.'

'I think we should go now, Mac. We're in a bad way. We might not start again, if we wait.'

A silence.

'Yes, we'll go now.'

They didn't go far. Within twenty feet the lassitude bore down on them again, heavier than ever. They were now literally crawling up the side of a mountain that seemed without end. And such was their paucity of strength that they clung claw-stiff, for minutes at a time, to any spur that offered more than minimal security against falling. At times the angle of ascent was greater than sixty degrees, and then they reached about them with ungainly, crippled limbs, in search of an easier passage. After a short while, they stopped once more.

'I am *old*,' grieved MacConnachie.

'Nonsense,' said Ansell.

Does it happen so quickly? thought MacConnachie. Does it come on a man so suddenly, and with so little warning? That he is one moment strong, and the next … We are finished. But so *quickly*.

It was not without warning. Last night, in the valley, we used the last of our strength. And last night, in the valley...

For this was the true root of his fear. He had told himself that he had failed to see the ambush because his eyes and ears were getting used up. But in truth he should have *known* it was there, because the gift should have told him. And the gift had not, because the gift itself was no longer there. It had been taken back.

He knew now what he had done to offend Nature. He had ruined Ansell; and that would not be forgiven him. You cannot go against Nature, and survive. She had taken back her gift because he no longer deserved it. That was just. It was proper. Retribution would be terrible, swift, and complete.

That he must die was plain, and he accepted it. But to die abandoned, that hurt.

Without the gift, he was just another man.

'It's no good, Mac. We'll have to rest.'

A long time, kid. A long time.

The rain came.

It fell with such violence, such completeness, that for a moment they were unable to take it in. In an instant the whole landscape turned fluid, the rock wall moved, and water poured past and down and around and beneath them, throwing up a gout of spume as though they sped upwards and the waters were still. They could see at once no more than a few feet in any direction. The air was full of falling water and tumultuous spray. The roaring of the torrent deafened them as rain thundered against their steel helmets and screeched over the stones.

The transformation was total.

And then pain came to them as driven rain embedded itself in ruined flesh. They lashed about in search of shelter. Ansell lost his footing and skittered down the slippery slope until the sodden material of his native coat caught among the glistening shards. His gun, transferred to his hand a moment before to ease his ravaged neck, flew from his grasp and twisted away out of sight into the roiling chasm below. And now the water tumbled down to find him, breaking against a spur just above him and showering his face with stinging, flinty persistence. He writhed and stretched in his efforts to avoid it, clinging at arm's length to the only crack his fingers could find, his eyes shut tight, his feet skidding and sliding off the stones as he sought desperately but in vain for further support.

Holding on for his life, MacConnachie peered down into the churning gloom, but nowhere could he see Ansell. The water poured over his clenched hand and down the sleeve of his coat but, since there was nothing in such soaked material to obstruct its passage, it flowed on across his chest and stomach to escape either along his other arm to the suitcase, or down his legs to his feet, where it overflowed his boots and reached the rock wall once again. The rain hammered against his back and neck, cascading off his steel helmet in blinding veils of liquid; his ears ached, and the skin of his cheeks throbbed. He tried to shout, but in the clamorous din he was unable even to hear himself.

He would have to go down.

I must have both hands free, he thought; but where to leave the case?

In an attempt to seek a fissure in the rock he turned back, but the rain, able once more to get at his face, attacked it savagely, blinding him. He tried to peer out through the gap where his lashes had once been, but it was useless; a jumping, poppled blur was all he could make out.

Resigning himself to blindness, he began to edge sideways through the racing water, acutely aware that one error of hand or foot might cause him to lose his tenuous contact with the rushing surface. He dragged the suitcase after him, dabbing out-wards with his other hand in search of a crack large enough to accommodate it; it wasn't until he had found one and raised himself with infinite caution to crouch over it that he perceived his mistake. The inferior material of the case had become so waterlogged that it had burst apart, torn open by the ragged edges of rock. Many of their possessions were gone, and a wet length of blanket trailed out beside him.

There was no time to worry about it. The crack he had found lay in the path of a tumbling stream that poured in at the top and swirled out at the bottom. But it was deep enough and, as far as he could judge, sufficiently jagged within to hold a bundle against the pressure of water. He stuffed the remains of the suitcase and its contents in as far as he could, forcing them down in an attempt to wedge them firmly.

The spout of water buffeted Ansell's ear until he screamed with pain. Again and again he turned his head in an attempt to avoid it, but to no avail. For minutes now he had been blind, and his arms and fingers had reached the point where even the fear of death would not long maintain their grip. He had succeeded in finding purchase for one foot, but every time he tried to use it to lever himself upwards the squishy leather of his boot slid off, and the entire weight of his body was thrown again on to his arms. The suddenness of his descent had pitched the canteen over his shoulder so that it now hung down his back. With each jerk the strap was closed more tightly about his throat; breathing was in any case difficult, for the water was always in his face. He feared that he might drown or suffocate before he fell. Of the three he preferred to fall; some part of his mind told him he must recognize the moment to decide.

MacConnachie, too, had come to understand that they were in danger of drowning. The ferocity of the downpour had thrown up a heavy, vaporous mist of spray thick as a curtain and many feet high; he was having to work his way downwards with painful and frightening slowness, and every time he took a gasp he swallowed as much water as he did air. He felt that his lungs were heavy with moisture and that he was, in reality, under water.

He struggled to keep going, wrenched and skidding often, every movement made rawly laborious by the weight of water with which he had to contend. But he could see nothing and he was tiring rapidly, as though the flowing streams drew the strength out of his old man's body and ran it useless down the mountain-side.

Then his feet made contact with a ledge and for a moment he rested, his body racked by a ruinous and chilling ague.

And there was Ansell beside him, not six inches away, clinging to a minute promontory, his feet dangling less than an inch above the security of the ledge. Why doesn't he let go and stand? he thought. Then he took hold of Ansell and caught him as he fell. He pressed the trembling body into the rock wall, covering it with his own, trying to warm and comfort it, trying to shelter his friend from the rain.

We must find shelter.

The sheer weight and volume of water was stunning, crushing and overwhelming them. A vast, wide, shallow river of rain poured down the face of the mountain, slashing into and over and through them as though it had no end and they were not there; wherever the fissures and splits in the rock formed any sort of line, wild, spurting jets had leapt into being, spouting up through the smaller crannies and roiling and bubbling and churning along until they lost themselves in the larger wash. The roaring of the tumult deafened them.

We must find shelter.

Ansell was sufficiently recovered to raise his face to

MacConnachie who, head bent against the violence of the storm, pointed upwards. Open-mouthed, Ansell nodded, and they set out; there was no point in wasting energy on a futile attempt to speak.

MacConnachie's first concern was to recover the suitcase. They could get no wetter, and the rain would not ease for a week; they could not afford to abandon their food for so long, assuming that it was still there, and that they could find it again.

It took an hour and forty-seven minutes to find it: one hundred and seven minutes of half-blind scrabbling about the treacherous slopes; and when they got there, more had gone. The tins remained, the knife, and the jars of paste and the bottle of oil; the blanket, fortunately, had snagged on a jagged edge so that, although it flared out beneath the mouth of the crack, it had not been carried away down the mountain. Everything else was lost to them: the razor, the kitchen knife, the tin of grease; the remnants of the suitcase and the piece of rope. The matches and candles, all were gone.

Between them, fumbling with cold fingers against the wet intractable material, they stuffed their remaining supplies into the pockets of their jackets and slacks. MacConnachie wrapped the sodden blanket round his neck, reaching under his native coat and pulling the ends down through the open top, and then tightening the belt to make sure that it couldn't escape.

Ansell followed MacConnachie in a wretched state of misery and confusion. He couldn't understand what had happened to the suitcase, or why they should make their desperate, scrambling ascent more difficult by burdening their pockets with hard-edged objects that bruised their thighs and chests. He remembered now the gun leaping from his grasp, and set to wondering how he might explain its loss. And then he thought, Mac has gone mad; he is rooting for truffles in the rain.

MacConnachie had found what he sought. If they went farther up the mountain-side they might find a better place, but he was now so cold and so tired that this would have to do.

It was a fissure large enough to accommodate both of them in some discomfort, with a gully at its mouth. Its upper edge protruded for about four feet, thus forming the roof of a small cavern in the rock. Where the roof ended the water poured over, but it was under sufficient pressure to be thrown clear of the cavern into the gully which, running down the angle of the slope, received the torrent and carried it away.

MacConnachie seized Ansell's coat and pushed him down into the fissure. Ansell ducked under the waterfall and disappeared from view; MacConnachie followed him into the protection of the rock.

Both were so exhausted that for some time they lay motionless, huddled together, neither thinking nor speaking, waiting for their increasingly sluggish recuperative powers to take effect.

Ansell had no idea how long he remained comatose but suddenly, to his surprise, he found his brain sharply alert. He was distressingly uncomfortable. The cavern was far smaller than he had thought and although, when he entered, he had coiled himself as tightly as he could against the back wall, the further entry of MacConnachie had squeezed him tighter yet. He wanted to move but the older man was breathing heavily and if he slept, he did not want to wake him. He found that, despite the raging of his wet burns, the condition that aggravated him most was the horrible, clammy embrace of his soaked clothing, and the juddering shivers it induced. With each onset of shaking a curious, low-pitched, quavering moan escaped from him, which he did nothing to produce and was powerless to arrest; in fact, it struck him as rather a funny sound and cheered him. So he

197

lay back, the contents of a sandwich between MacConnachie and the rock, suspended between amusement and suffering, taking a long view of their predicament.

Time passed and, the state of suspension fading, he began to take note of their shelter. There was a fair degree of light made flickering by the steady passage of water outside, and he bent to look at MacConnachie. The eyes were open, but without intelligence. He looked again towards the curtain of water in the doorway and, by virtue of this, perhaps, and the spattering and gurgling in the gully, he was seized by an urgent desire to urinate.

'Christ!'

In a panic he tried to rise, knocked his head, and vomited on to MacConnachie's legs; at the same moment, he peed into his trousers. Then a spasm shook his whole body and he became once more still. He saw that MacConnachie's eyes were on him.

'Sorry about that.'

He brushed vaguely at the mess which, difficult to distinguish from the general sogginess, seemed far less than it had felt.

'Doesn't matter.'

'I peed in my trousers.'

MacConnachie took his hand.

'Not wet enough already?'

Ansell put his other hand on to MacConnachie's, holding Mac's one hand with both of his. He said,

'How do you feel?'

'A hundred years old.'

'You don't look a day over ninety-nine.'

The faintest smile appeared on MacConnachie's face. Ansell touched his lips.

'We ought to take these damned helmets off.'

'Yes.'

MacConnachie looked so uncomfortable with the strap under

his chin, his head canted to one side by the lower steel rim, that Ansell inserted his fingers under the canvas and began to ease it over MacConnachie's jaw. Then he stopped.

'Mac.'

'What?'

'It's stuck.'

'How?'

'In the gug under your chin.'

A slight frown.

'But it's wet.'

'It's still stuck.' Ansell reached up. 'So's mine.'

'You'd better pull it off.'

'Okay.'

Ansell took hold of the chin-strap again and gave it a sharp jerk. There was a slight tearing feeling but MacConnachie's expression didn't change; it was as though he hadn't felt it. Then Ansell eased his other hand under the spongy roll of blanket about MacConnachie's neck, raised his head, took the helmet off and lay it crown down under the back of MacConnachie's head as a pillow. MacConnachie shut his eyes, relaxing:

'Ah, that's better.'

'Good.'

MacConnachie's hand still lay in his lap as Ansell reached up again, ungummed his own strap and removed his helmet. He rubbed the top of his head.

'If we still had hair, it would be dry.'

'That's a thought.'

The rain pounded down outside. Another spasm of shivering passed through Ansell.

'What happened to the case?'

'It came apart.'

'I lost my gun.'

'It doesn't matter.'

Ansell had taken hold of MacConnachie's hand again.

'What are we going to do, Mac?'

'I don't know.' MacConnachie stared at the roof a few feet above his head. 'I'd meant to move during the rain, while the chopper couldn't get up. Now, I don't know.'

'How long will it last?'

'Three weeks.'

'We can't wait that long.'

'It'll ease after a week.'

'We can't wait that long either.'

'No.'

'Excreta Avenue.'

'Excreta Avenue it is.'

A silence.

'What have we left?'

'Soup, two tins. Paste, two jars.'

'And water.'

'There's plenty of that.'

'That's all.'

'That's all.'

Ansell thought. The whole adventure had begun to take on a curious unreality now, as though the sharpness of apprehension occupied, after all, only the surface of the mind; and just below, in unhurried patience, lay the realities of confusion and absurdity, waiting their turn. It would come. Time was with them. He said,

'Just down the slope—about a hundred feet—there's a group of Goons in ambush. With food.'

'So?'

'We can steal their food.'

'In this?'

'When it eases up.'

'It won't ease up for long enough. Anyway, we haven't the strength or the fire power. They're fit and armed.'

'We can't last long on what we've got.'

'So it's a question of whether we die up here, or down there.'

'We can try.'

'What's the point?'

'Come to that, what's the point of any of it?'

A faint smile on MacConnachie's face.

'Damned if I know.'

Silence.

'Why don't we give ourselves up?'

'I suppose I'd sooner be here than there.'

Silence.

'We've got to do something.'

'It must be something we can do.'

'All the time we get weaker.'

'Then what we do must be easier.'

A silence.

'I could go.'

MacConnachie's eyes flickered towards him, then back to the roof.

'Kid, when the times comes, do as you like. I'll go or stay, whatever you want.'

Silence.

'Can we do nothing?'

'Nothing.'

'It seems a pity after—all this.'

'It is.'

Silence.

'It's cold in here.

'It'll get colder.'

Ansell sat abstractedly. Then,

'They're sitting down there. Not more than thirty yards away. They can't move, and we can't. It's funny. They don't even know we're here.'

'I hope the bastards forgot their tents.'

The rain stopped, and started again. Night fell. Ansell said,

'When I was a child, I used to dream about being safe from the rain, in a hole, under the bedclothes, crouched down. It isn't like that.'

When dawn came the rain was still falling, on the eighth day. MacConnachie felt stronger, but he was very cold and wet, and couldn't detect the warmth in his own body. Ansell, who lay slumped against his right arm and side, felt warmer; but it may simply have been that, where their bodies touched, they were able to generate between them sufficient heat for one. He tried to extricate himself without waking Ansell, but Ansell said,

'What's the time?'

'Just after dawn.'

'It's still raining.'

MacConnachie, hunching himself round in the gloomy enclosure, said,

'I know. This may sound stupid, but I'm going to have a pee.'

Ansell, disposing his body to accommodate MacConnachie's new position, said,

'Good idea. I'll have one after you.'

MacConnachie raised his native coat, opened his trousers, and hobbled forward on his knees until he was within a few inches of the falling water to add his quota to it. As his bladder emptied, a crippling pain rose from his loins into his stomach so that he had to bend forward to master it, but at length it passed and the flow ended. Ansell said,

'That was a long one.'

MacConnachie said,

'God, that hurt, but I feel better for it.'

Clambering over one another they exchanged positions and Ansell, too, relieved himself. He said,

'I wonder if we'll ever do the other again.'

'Not through over-eating we won't.'

Rather than change positions yet again, they settled as they were.

There was a silence.

Then Ansell looked at MacConnachie.

'Do I smell?'

'I don't know, kid. I can't smell a thing.'

'We must smell, Mac. We must smell awful. I peed myself yesterday.'

'I shouldn't worry. You can't smell any worse than I do.'

But MacConnachie had missed the tense solemnity of Ansell's tone. Now Ansell said,

'But we do smell, Mac. My hands ... Look at us. We're horrible!' And suddenly his voice rose to a terrible, strangulated cry: 'Christ, Jesus, we're animals! We're—*monsters*!'

It was true. Ansell's puffed eyeholes burned with supplication and grief. His wizened old head was cocked in simian anguish. So quickly had the crisis arisen that MacConnachie was unprepared. Then he reached forward and took hold of Ansell.

'It's all right, kid, it's all right.'

'What have we *done*?'

'It's okay.'

'What have we *done* to ourselves?'

'It's all right, kid, don't worry.'

'Oh Christ, God, Jesus ...

'It's all right, it's all right, it's all right ... '

And MacConnachie rocked Ansell until he stopped crying.

'Sorry. That was stupid.'

'Doesn't matter.'

'It was the pee on my fingers, the thought of it.'

'We do look pretty awful.'

Ansell was staring at his finger-tips.

'They look like an old tramp's gloves. Only it isn't ragged wool, it's flesh.'

'Our mothers wouldn't know us.'

'It was like seeing us as we are. For the first time.'

'Yeah, well ... We've got each other for a mirror.'

Ansell looked surprised at so exact a remark from MacConnachie. Then he said,

'I suppose we ought to eat something.'

MacConnachie tried to smile encouragingly.

'That's it. Order of the day. Nosh.'

While MacConnachie fumbled to open a soup tin with the fish knife, their only remaining knife, Ansell watched him. He thought, his fingers must be stinging like my own now that the rain has washed the crust away. He looked again at his finger-tips. They are so pinky-white, he thought, so bloodless, like sponge. Then, with the first shock and horror of their appearance now reduced to an enormity that quietly burned within, he fell to examining MacConnachie in confirmation of himself.

The body was shapeless, squat in the cavern, wrapped about by the dank stiff folds of the native coat. The head hung lower than the shoulders, which were hunched. The arms sprouted incongruously from the dark mass, the clumsy hands naked, claw-like and shredded. All over the face and pate dangled tiny strips of dead flesh that waved with each movement in imitation of a sea anemone. The surface covering was drawn tight against the bones and yet it displayed in texture a curious anomaly, seeming both stiff and soggy at the same time. There was no discernible colour; simply a dead white, bruised and riven with shadow. Where the eyes had been, there were deep black craters that might have been painted in. In places the skin appeared to have melted, travelling down towards and over the neck as the wax of a candle dribbles down its stem. The mouth was a hole drawn straight across; a crack; a mistake. The ears were ravaged beyond repair; only the nose was human, hooked and unmistakable.

Is this what we come to? A nose? he thought. If only the brain could be damaged in concert with the body; if only their rates of deterioration could be synchronized, how much more bearable life would be.

But then, perhaps they are.

It may have been the lack of space, or the gloom, or the damage to his hands, but MacConnachie was having the utmost difficulty in piercing the top of the tin. Every time he raised the knife and brought it down it skidded off, or he missed the tin entirely, or caught its edge and drove it over on to its side; once he stabbed himself lightly in the thigh, but he withdrew the blade apparently unaware, and time and again he missed the hand that held the tin only by chance. All the while he swore persistently and despairingly. For some time Ansell watched this operation before, shocked at the lag in his reactions, he grasped the other side of the tin.

'Let me help.'

'Thanks.'

The blade rose and fell three more times, skittering about the metal surface as MacConnachie's wrist tired, and then the point penetrated with a small hiss.

'Thank God for that.'

MacConnachie threw the knife aside. Ansell said,

'We need two holes, Mac.'

'What?'

'Two holes.'

'Oh Christ!'

MacConnachie seized the knife again and drove it up and down

205

in a frantic, cross tattoo until the metal buckled and split once more.

'Next question,' he said, throwing it away again.

'How do you like your consommé?'

'Cold.'

'How fortunate. It happens to be the speciality of the house.'

MacConnachie laughed slightly.

'You have half, then I will.'

Ansell took the tin between both his hands, raised it to his mouth and sucked some of the thick liquid down; it had an odd taste that puzzled him.

'What is it?'

'I don't know. What does it say on the label?'

'The label's gone.'

'Can't you remember?'

'No.'

'Guess then.

Ansell drew in some more and tested it against his palate, swallowing, and smacking his tongue against the roof of his mouth. MacConnachie said, 'Well?'

Ansell pondered then, as might a connoisseur, and finally pronounced:

'Cream of Chicken.'

'We're living like kings!'

But the soup was like a ribbon of chill worming its way deep into his guts, and he quickly became nauseated. He handed the tin to MacConnachie, who sucked eagerly, looked startled, spat and exclaimed,

'Christ, it's horrible!'

There was a silence. Ansell shivered.

'Have we no way to make fire?'

'None that I know of.'

'I wonder if they've got fire down the hill.'

'There's nothing we can do about it if they have. Not yet.'

MacConnachie tilted the tin once more, but then even he had had enough. Ansell said,

'I hate just sitting here, doing nothing.'

'We'll have to do something soon enough.'

'What?'

A pause.

'I'll tell you when the time comes.'

Ansell said nothing. MacConnachie held out the tin.

'Here, finish it.'

'I don't want it.'

'Finish it.'

'Stuff it.'

'All right, suit yourself.'

MacConnachie threw the tin out through the sheet of rain. For a long time they sat silent, then MacConnachie said,

'Don't let me down now. I couldn't have got this far without you.'

'Neither could I.'

MacConnachie said:

'If we attack the Goons, there are too many. And we've still got a chance. When the time comes, we'll know. Then, each man decides for himself. But at the moment, we've still got a chance. We have.'

'Yes, Mac.'

'We have.'

'Yes, Mac.'

A long pause.

'We have.'

Time passed. Ansell thought, it's extraordinary how you get used to the rain all the time, as you get used to the sickness and the pain. They fall on you from the sky, and in the end you don't notice them.

'It'll be night soon.'
Ansell blinked.
'Already?'
'The day's gone.'
'I didn't see.'
A pause.
'Shall we eat?'
'I don't mind.'
'It doesn't matter.'

Some time during the night, Ansell said,
'We're waiting for death, aren't we?'
'We won't just wait, kid. I promise you that. We'll go to meet it.'
A silence.
'I'm sorry, Mac.'
'Don't be.'
'You really wanted to get away, didn't you?'
A pause.
'Didn't you?'
A pause.
'I'm happy to be with you.'
MacConnachie strove, with all his strength, that Ansell might not hear the dry, tearless sobs that racked him.

Ansell thought that MacConnachie might be laughing, but he didn't mind. After a time, he said,
'Tell me about the women.'
There was a silence, then MacConnachie's voice:
'We need 'em. Don't let anyone kid you. A woman is ... soft ... and ... What they give. The crappiest old tart. They smell

good. They've got hair. You. You can hide ... in a woman. The best of them. There's no ... fear ... where a woman is. You poke a woman ... there's no ... *fear*.'

The voice stopped.

'Sounds all right,' said Ansell.

Towards dawn, MacConnachie said,

'But we *are* free! We *are* free!'

'Yes, Mac. We're free.'

Ansell dozed, and in his dreams he had a woman. His first. He couldn't remember the dream, but he woke up different; more peaceful.

It was the ninth day, and MacConnachie was already awake.

'We must move soon. It is time.'

'Yes. I'm ready.'

'Good. We'll have a pee. And some soup. And when the rain stops ... '

'We'll go out.'

'Into the open. Yes.'

But all that day it rained.

Ansell said,

'Shall we go on up the hill? Or shall we attack the Goons?'

'What do you want to do?'

'I want to go on up the hill. I don't want to—not be free again.'

'I want to—go up the hill, too.'

'Good. That's settled, then.'

'It's funny.'

'What is?'

'I don't know. All of it. Funny.'

'Die laughing.'

'In some places, you know, they hold on to their slashers all the time, because they're afraid they'll fly up into their stomachs like a piece of elastic.'

'In others, they call that pocket billiards.

A discernibly giggly sound came from Ansell.

'What's the matter?'

'That's funny.'

'What is?'

'Pocket billiards.'

'Christ.'

'Actually, I don't think they have pockets.'

It was bitterly cold that night. Huddled together, no longer hungry or properly sensible, they waited for the rain to stop and for the dawn to come. Ansell felt, as he never had before, that the cold came from *inside* him. Normally, when a man is cold, it is his extremities that ache, and from within a warm glow reaches out to sustain him; but now his finger-tips and ears were warmer than his stomach, which lay within him leaden, heavy and chill. The spark of life had moved, as though it were on its way out; a curious phenomenon. He said,

'One day ... '

After a time, MacConnachie said,

'What?'

There was a silence, and then Ansell started to hum:

'Show me the way to go home,
I'm tired and I want to go to bed,
I had a little drink about an hour ago,
And it's gone right ... to ... my ... head ... '

MacConnachie said,

'Don't worry, kid. It won't be bad. Not bad.'

'I'm not worried, Mac.'

It's what a man comes to, anyway, thought MacConnachie.

But when it came, it was bad.

Dawn on the tenth day. They performed their ritual of peeing, and then drank the last tin of soup which, by some oversight, they had failed to consume the previous day. An hour after dawn, the rain stopped. MacConnachie looked out.

'We might as well go.'

'Yes.'

MacConnachie looked at him, and shrugged.

'It's a day for it.'

'Yes.'

MacConnachie crawled stiffly out and Ansell followed. By mutual unspoken consent they left their helmets behind. Ansell thought: this is pointless, really; we'd be far better off in the cave. He found himself humming again: 'You'd be far better off in a Home.' We don't need helmets where we're going, by all accounts. 'Ladies and gentlemen, I have the great pleasure of introducing to you tonight Professor MacConnachie, who has recently returned from a long journey to the Other World.' Applause.

Who wants to die in a cave?

They crawled high-bottomed up the mountain-side. Rivulets and little streams trickled and chuckled and gurgled down the cracks in the shining slopes. The air was heavy with moisture.

'... and in conclusion, I should like to pay tribute to my faithful bearer and drum-beater, Basher Ansell, without whom ...' Applause. Come now. A man who is about to die should harbour more solemn thoughts. Long live the Holy Mother of

God! Applause again. I wonder if mine would have been a virgin? Go on, now pull the other one.

It's got bells on.

When the rain started again they were still crawling. Keep going, MacConnachie thought; just keep going, that's all. The blinding sheets of water wrapped about and enfolded them, enclosing them in a fast-dribbling blanket. The river ran down the mountain-side, pressing between their fingers, seeking always to render their grasp untenable. At length, blundering upon another hole, MacConnachie crawled into it, turned and pulled Ansell after him.

It was little more than a large crack in the rock wall, far from being habitable. Water lay inches deep in the bottom, but they settled down and waited for the rain to stop. At some point in the night, Ansell said,
'Are we still alive?'

On the eleventh day, when day had come, but how long since MacConnachie didn't know, he found that he was grasping a jar paw-like between his padded hands, licking the paste therein, and puzzling that it had so conveniently lost its lid; he had no recollection of having removed it. Remembering that he was not alone, he passed the jar to Ansell who, letting it fall into the water, nuzzled about for some time with snout and pads before he lost interest.

The rain stopped, and they started to crawl again. Upwards at first; and then, although they were unaware of the fact, sideways along the line of an ill-defined ledge in the rock. For a while, the sun showed weakly and the stone glowed wetly back.

It was here, minutes or days later, that the helicopter found them.

MacConnachie became aware of the roaring presence. From his hands and knees he rolled over on to his bottom. He sought out the bottle of oil. With the gun laid across his legs, he tried to unscrew the top but failed. All the while, the helicopter hovered overhead. At length, with his teeth, MacConnachie managed to open the bottle and spat the cap away. The pilot, he knew, was trying to decide whether to kill them or attempt to recapture them. This, what I am doing, is important, he thought; but it's taking such a hell of a stupid long time.

He opened the working parts of the gun and poured the remainder of the oil in, throwing the bottle away. He then dabbled his fingers in the breech, running them over the rust-brown metal of the weapon. A shot cracked dully up above, and the ricochet sang off near by. He operated the working parts until they slid smoothly, ejecting four or five rounds, then lay back to take aim. Ansell said,

'They're shooting at us.'

A burst was fired from above and MacConnachie felt his leg leap as bullets hit his foot. The other rounds jumped on the rock, throwing up powdered scree. MacConnachie fired single shots, grouped together in two bunches of three. They smacked against the frontage—one might have penetrated—and the helicopter rose up out of range.

Then the sun went in and the chopper fell quickly away from them. A moment later it started to rain again.

'He's taking his chances,' said MacConnachie, sitting up and lying forward over the gun in his lap to protect it. He found that he was looking at his foot. Ansell said,

'It certainly concentrates the mind, quite wonderfully.'

MacConnachie saw that his boots were tinted green and one upper had at last come adrift from the sole. Glancing across, he saw that Ansell's boots were worse, being badly cracked. He looked again at the foot that had been hit but, apart from two neat punctures, there was nothing to see. Ansell said,

'Does it hurt?'

'No. I think it's already dead.'

'Ah.'

The rain was still quite light, as though waiting for them to finish speaking. MacConnachie said,

'We mustn't let them take us alive.'

'No.'

'Must—stay awake—long enough to be killed.'

'Yes.'

'It's important.'

'Yes. Hate to miss it.'

And then the rain drowned every other noise.

Stop laughing, Ansell told himself.

MacConnachie lay slumped forward over the gun, trying to keep it dry for the next encounter, patient, waiting, at peace, the water running off his head.

Does it hurt, indeed? Only when I laugh. Why not bite on the bullet? Oh Christ, Christ, Christ, Christ, Christ...

Time passed.

Daylight.

The rain stopped.

'New magazine,' said MacConnachie.

Ansell fumbled out a fresh magazine. MacConnachie dropped the other, although there were rounds left in it. Fingers too blunt to reload individual bullets. Ansell fixed the full magazine to the gun. The helicopter came again.

This time it came firing as soon as it was in range. But not too close. Testing us out, thought MacConnachie: is there life in the bastards yet? Come a little closer, my friend, and see for yourself.

MacConnachie held his fire. I want him. Oh God, I want him

like I never wanted anything. It isn't much to ask. To take that bastard with me.

The chopper rose up the slope with the ponderous movement of a lift, spraying bullets in short bursts, always a little closer to their bodies, awaiting a reaction. MacConnachie had lain back full length again. When it was close enough, he fired. The perspex cracked somewhere near the pilot's feet, then split and shattered. The observer fired back. Particles of stone flew about and Ansell let out a little cry of surprise. The chopper tilted and rose up sharply. MacConnachie grunted with pleasure. Ansell said, 'My hand.'

MacConnachie took a quick look: Ansell's left hand hung awry, shattered at the wrist.

Then the helicopter came again from behind and above—Ah Christ, it hurts to turn my head that far—a sputtering snout, bullets everywhere, jumping, singing, smacking on the rock. In a daze, MacConnachie fired at the muzzle flash. The weapon tilted; a hand jerked up to an eye as though pulled on a string. MacConnachie realigned his own gun and put two more shots through the crack as the chopper passed overhead before dropping once more away down the mountain-side.

Crash, damn you, crash.

'New magazine.'
Ansell was holding his broken arm.
'Yes.'
He searched about under his clothing, then said,
'I haven't got one.'
'Pocket.'
Ansell fumbled about until he found another magazine in MacConnachie's slacks pocket, which he handed to him. MacConnachie changed magazines and said,
'Put that one back.'
Ansell put the half-empty magazine into the pocket from which the full one had come. MacConnachie said,

'How's your hand?'

'Sort of numb.'

MacConnachie looked into the sky.

'He'll come again soon.'

'I wish they'd get it done with.'

'They will.'

Silence.

'Will they come up from below?'

'Now. Yes.'

A silence.

'You get so you lose interest.'

'You must stay awake.'

MacConnachie waited. He thought perhaps the pilot hadn't told about finding them the first time, but now he would have to, with yet another dead navigator to explain away.

I wish to God, thought Ansell, they'd kill us. Just come and just kill us.

The helicopter came again. Straight at them. Firing burst after burst. Hovering, firing, hovering, firing, turning, firing, coming from behind, firing. MacConnachie fired back, desperate to enlarge that crack, splitting and tearing his skin in an attempt to follow the cumbrous movements of the aircraft. Go down, go down, GO DOWN!

Bullets poured into MacConnachie, slashing across his chest, churning his stomach, smashing his rib-cage to pieces. Dimly, he heard Ansell cry out. He half rose, foundered, fell to his knees, rolled on to his side. GO DOWN, GO DOWN, GO DOWN. He wrenched the gun up and fired again. He tried to get to his feet. Bullets thudded into his back, or it might have been the rain. His mouth was full of thick, hot liquid. He rose to his feet. The helicopter was very close, all muddied and smudged with dark stains and darting, cobweb shadows. He fired his gun from the hip. The helicopter came so close he fell again and fired up into its underbelly.

He rose to his hands and knees, and fell against Ansell. Ansell had the gun in the crook of his good arm and was firing upwards from the hip.

Ansell had been hit in the thigh. When he saw MacConnachie totter and spin, he lost his bearings for a moment; then Mac-Connachie was grovelling in pink slime, and the gun lay at his feet. Ansell had picked it up. There was dark slobber dripping from MacConnachie's chin. Ansell fired as the chopper drifted in towards them again and the recoil knocked him on to his bottom.

Then the rain came, and the helicopter went away.

One thing about the rain, it washed MacConnachie clean. Ansell felt very calm. MacConnachie looked—*flatter*. Yes, flatter. His lips were moving. Ansell leaned forward to put his ear close.

'Get—him,' said MacConnachie.

'Of course,' said Ansell, who might have been replying to a child's request for the moon.

After a long time, MacConnachie's lips moved again, and Ansell again leant close.

'Fresh magazine.'

Ansell found one, at length, in MacConnachie's bush jacket. It was all very damp and crumpled under there. But it was wet, anyway.

MacConnachie was speaking again.

'Don't let them ... '

Ansell waited. Finally, he said,

'No.'

The rain stopped. Ansell thought that by sitting on Mac-Connachie's stomach he might protect him a little. Anyway, he did, and the helicopter came again.

This time, it didn't fire.
Come on, for God's sake. What is this? A game?
But it sat up there in the sky and it didn't fire.
What do I *do*?

They want to take you alive, kid. Be careful. Look down.

And then Ansell saw them coming up the mountain towards him. Ah, no. God, no. I can't—do it—myself.

They came slowly up, cautiously, waiting to see what he would do. He fired at them but they didn't fire back. They went to cover, waiting.

After a long time they started to move, but when he fired they went to cover again.

They had all the time.

Give me the gun, kid.

Ansell felt MacConnachie's hand claw weakly at his waist. He turned round.

'What?'

MacConnachie seemed to be reaching for the gun. Ansell smiled.

'You've done your share.'

But MacConnachie went on reaching for it, a look of intense pleading in his eyes. Ansell smiled again.

'All right.'

He took hold of MacConnachie's battered hand and wrapped it round the gun, helping him to thread his ruined finger through the trigger guard.

'There.'

MacConnachie relaxed a moment, closing his eyes, the picture of satisfaction; Ansell smiled to have given him such pleasure.

Then he felt the snout nuzzle against his side, for he had turned his back. He turned again to MacConnachie. Very slowly, effortfully, MacConnachie was raising the gun higher, his eyes burning with a great longing and pain.

Ansell felt that he had always known why MacConnachie wanted the gun. He turned properly so that he could face MacConnachie. He took hold of the barrel of the gun to help him, raising it to his own face.

'Thank you, Mac,' he said. And then,

'Thank you.'

He put the muzzle into his mouth, closed his eyes, and gripped it tightly.

MacConnachie shut his eyes. It's damn-all I've done for you, kid. But I love you, see? I love you. He pulled the trigger.

They all seemed to have gone mad. There was a pink spray. The helicopter jumped. They came running up the hill towards him. He fired and fired again. They stood around and fired into him. Ansell's body toppled off.

Fuck you all, he said.

Fuck you all.

You should see it, kid. It's all mountains. Far as the eye can see. Mountains!

Laugh.

We'd never have got